SOLD TO THE DUKE

JOANNA SHUPE

Copyright © 2021 by Joanna Shupe

Originally published in the *Rake I'd Like to F...* anthology, November 2021.

All rights reserved.

No part of this book may be reproduced in any form or by any electronic or mechanical means, including information storage and retrieval systems, without written permission from the author, except for the use of brief quotations in a book review.

This is a work of fiction. Any names or characters, businesses or places, events or incidents, are fictitious. Any resemblance to actual persons, living or dead, or actual events is purely coincidental.

Cover: Letitia Hasser, RBA Designs

Editing: Sabrina Darby

CHAPTER 1

THE CHAPEL, LONDON, 1895

A stranger was about to bid on her body, for the right to take what should belong to a husband.

But Eliza had no husband, nor did she want one. What she wanted was money—a lot of it.

Most people didn't understand desperation. Not true desperation, the kind that sat in one's belly, rotten and relentless, dragging a person down into a pit of despair. Over the last year, as her sister grew sicker, Eliza had come to know desperation well. Too well, in fact. She was drowning in it, completely out of decent options.

Which left her with only indecent options.

The Chapel auctions were legendary in certain segments of London, whispered about on the streets, with women bragging of the money to be had and the chance to find a wealthy protector. After thinking on it for months, Eliza finally submitted her name, agreeing to auction herself off.

Please, let him be kind.

"Cor, you look bloody nervous." A woman sat next to Eliza. "Is this your first time, love? It won't be as bad as that."

Eliza swallowed and wrapped her arms around herself. They'd given all the women a simple white shift to wear, the fabric nearly transparent. "Yes, it's my first auction." *My first everything.*

The woman's brows rose slightly at hearing Eliza's accent, which still held hints of Mayfair. "What's a fancy dove like you doing here?"

"Same as everyone else. I need the money."

The woman struck out her hand. "I'm Helen."

They shook hands. "Eliza."

"Nice to meet you, Eliza. This is my third time. You'll be fine. Just do as he asks for seven nights and then you'll go home with a fat purse full of coin."

Seven nights.

A cold prickle of fear snaked down Eliza's spine. For seven nights she would be at the mercy of a stranger with unlimited rights to her person.

This was your choice. You knew what you were agreeing to.

If there was any other option, she would take it. But she had a younger sister to consider, one who would die without treatment. This required money—and Eliza did not want to become a mistress, always at the mercy of a man's whims. Her current predicament notwithstanding, she wanted to keep her independence, which was why the auction was perfect. Seven nights, then she was free.

"Never heard of a cruel bidder," Helen was saying. "The Chapel's owner is particular about who he lets attend. It's why the women are so eager to get a spot each month." She patted Eliza's knee. "Stay bricky and you'll be fine."

Eliza drew in a deep breath. No matter what happened, she would be fine, wouldn't she? She'd survive this, as she had everything else.

She'd survived the death of her parents, as well as the death of her brother, Robert.

She'd survived being cast out with only a few possessions by the new earl, their second cousin and Robert's successor.

She and her sister had survived the streets, the uncertainty. The hunger. Demeaning jobs for meager wages.

Eliza would survive this, too.

It's only your body. No one can touch your heart or your mind.

For one week, she could do anything if it helped Fanny get better.

"Thank you," she murmured to Helen gratefully.

"You're welcome. Oh, and go see the midwife for some pennyroyal at the end of the week. The kind that prevents consequences."

"My neighbor suggested cotton root tea." Martha worked in a bordello, and she'd filled Eliza in on what to expect after the auction. According to Martha, intimacies with a man were generally pleasurable, if not downright addicting. Eliza figured it must be true, considering all the babies in the world.

In the last five years, Eliza had seen and heard quite a lot. Knife fights, opium addicts, pickpockets . . .and yes, sexual favors. The alleys were full of all kinds of grunts and groans, people desperate for physical release.

Most of Eliza's education, however, came from their former neighbors, who'd been loud and enthusiastic in their intimacies, not to mention very specific about what they liked. Thanks to thin walls, Eliza wasn't completely ignorant as to what would occur during these seven nights.

Truthfully, she was looking forward to ridding herself of her innocence. Eliza didn't have time for courting—those dreams died long ago, about the time she cleaned her first privy—but she would like to be held, to experience true pleasure, and to pleasure someone in return. Someone to fulfill these *urges* that haunted her at night, the physical cravings that had her reaching underneath the bedclothes to touch between her legs. . . .

Being a virgin was lonely and exhausting.

"Yes," Helen said, "cotton root tea works too, though I think the pennyroyal tastes better."

Before she could thank Helen again, the side door opened and the room fell silent. A woman holding a journal entered and began reading names. It was the same woman who'd signed Eliza up for the auction. Each auction participant answered when her name was called.

"Eliza," the woman said.

"Here," Eliza said in the loudest voice she could muster.

"Are you still a virgin, love?"

The air seemed to disappear out of the room as every head swung her way. "Yes."

The woman nodded once and closed her journal. "Ladies, we'll begin shortly."

Then she left, leaving the women alone, and Eliza's skin burned. Everyone here now knew she was innocent.

"A virgin," Helen said, her voice full of wonder, as if Eliza had declared herself a mermaid. "Bloomin' hell. You're going to fetch a fortune."

* * *

HANDS WERE EVERYWHERE.

Lucien groaned, lust heavy in his blood, like a drug weighing down his veins. The carriage had stopped ages ago and he truly didn't wish to break up this lovely party...but he'd promised.

"My darlings," he said gently, trying to gain the attention of his distracted companions. Delicate fingers slid inside his trousers to stroke his hard cock through his underclothes, and he groaned. Ginny was sliding to her knees, a devilish twinkle in her eye, while Mollie pushed her bare breast deeper into Lucien's hand. He tweaked her nipple, unable to help himself.

"Your Grace needn't attend this auction," Ginny cooed as her fingers started on the buttons of his undergarment. "We are perfectly happy seeing to your needs."

How well he knew this. Ginny and Mollie were delightful in every way, the two actresses having been his regular bed partners for three months. Their time together had been a blur of orgasms and sensual spankings, but he'd promised Jasper, his closest friend, that he'd attend tonight.

"I'm not bidding on a girl." Reluctantly, he covered Mollie's abundant tits with her dress. "Nevertheless, my presence has been requested."

While Lucien avoided the auctions, preferring to get women through natural charm, Jasper attended often. Unfortunately, Jasper had terrible taste in people—hence their friendship—and was no stranger to getting fleeced by unscrupulous women. He'd begged for Lucien's help in selecting a girl tonight, and Lucien hadn't been able to refuse.

Mollie's lips met the edge of his ear. "Wouldn't you rather fuck me up the bum instead?"

A rush of need surged inside him, his cock pulsing as if pleading for Lucien to follow through on the suggestion. *Damn it.*

Lucien closed his eyes and dug deep for control. Once he had a grip on himself, he helped Ginny up off the floor and began righting his clothing. The girls laughed as his fingers fumbled on the task, his haste and hunger making him clumsy.

He pressed a long, deep kiss to Mollie's mouth, then gave Ginny the same. "I won't be long, loves. You may wait here or the house in Cheapside. I'll find you after."

Before they could argue or tempt him further, he alighted from the carriage. The cool night air slapped his overheated skin and he willed his erection away. Aware of the rules for auction nights, he removed the domino from his coat pocket and slipped it over his face. Then he straightened his shoulders and walked toward the club, determined to get this over with as quickly as possible.

The smell of sweat and desperation hung heavy inside, the interior of the club crowded with men clad in evening suits and masks, each hoping to win a woman for seven nights. *Fools.*

"I was beginning to wonder if you were coming," said a voice behind him.

Annoyed, Lucien turned to his friend. "Have you any idea what you've interrupted? This had better not take long."

"Your mistresses, I know. Don't worry. You'll help me win a woman and then we shall all go our separate ways."

"Why do you keep bidding on these women if you can't trust them?"

"That's what I need you for. The last woman I won here stole two of my favorite paintings."

Christ, Jasper was too trusting by half. "You are hopeless."

"Yes, absolutely. But if anyone knows women, it's you. Please, you must help me, Luc." Jasper clapped him on the shoulder, pushing Lucien through the doorway. "Just sit down. I'll have you out of here shortly."

Instead of arguing, Lucien continued into the room. An empty table along the side seemed as good as any, so Lucien sat and surveyed the crowd. The masks provided appallingly little anonymity, and he could identify most everyone here, the titled gents and rich industrialists who frequented all the same clubs and theaters.

He had to hand it to the owner. These auctions were quite the rage. To participate, a man required someone respectable to vouch for him, and any hint of violence in one's past was just cause for refusal. This meant women came willingly, eager to be auctioned, and they received every quid of the auction price paid. The owners knew the real money was in the exorbitant participation fee and the liquor sold when the room was packed.

Lucien ordered drinks for them both and relaxed. Within minutes, movement from behind the curtain caught his eye. The audience quieted, anticipation thick like fog in the room.

A large barrel-chested man stepped out onto the stage. "Owner of the Chapel," Jasper whispered to Lucien.

The owner, who looked like a dockside worker, gave a speech about how the auction would proceed, the rules for how the women were to be treated, and the consequences for those who disobeyed the rules. Lucien had little doubt that those consequences were doled out by the owner himself, whose hands could probably snap a smaller man in half.

The auction began. Woman after woman was paraded on the stage as men shouted their bids. Jasper settled on a cheeky-looking blond beauty somewhere along the way.

"May I leave now?" Lucien asked after Jasper was declared the winning bidder.

"No. You must meet her, just to see if she's going to give me trouble."

Though eager to bolt, Lucien sighed and forced himself to stay seated. Only for Jasper would Lucien postpone a night of glorious fucking and debauchery.

Bored by the auction proceedings, he studied the crowd. Odd, but several men here hadn't bid at all, their hawkish gazes never leaving the stage. Rathbone was one, a marquess who, according to Mollie, had sexual tastes that skewed toward the macabre. Something about cutting the insides of Mollie's friend's thighs before he fucked her—as she pretended to be a corpse. Has word not gotten around about Rathbone? Curious that he'd been allowed to participate tonight.

Lucien leaned over to Jasper. "I've heard some unsavory stories about Rathbone. Surprised to see him here."

"Unsavory? Rathbone? I've never heard any hint of that."

"Mollie has a friend, said he—"

"And now," the auctioneer said, "we have our final offering for the night. Gents, I give you, Lady E."

The curtains parted and a pale young woman slowly emerged. She was lovely, with golden blond hair piled atop her head, wisps surrounding her delicate face. Bright blue eyes surveyed the crowd nervously, her body shaking in a clear case of nerves. She couldn't have been more than nineteen or twenty.

The shift she wore did little to cover her. Dusky nipples, furled into hard points thanks to the cold air and lack of undergarments, poked the thin fabric, the small swell of her breasts evident. She had long bony legs, thin arms, and he could see a hint of dark hair covering her mound.

Something nagged in his brain at the sight of her. Why did she look vaguely familiar? The auctioneer took the girl's hand and led her around the stage, like a prized stallion at Tattersall's. Lucien couldn't tear his gaze away, knowing there was something about her. Something he couldn't finger. A puzzle he couldn't quite solve.

"Lady E is the Chapel's most special offering," the man crowed. "Genteel, mannered, and best of all . . .a virgin."

A collective gasp went through the room.

"That's right, gents. This lovely creature has never had a man between her thighs. Whoever wins her for seven nights will be her first."

Color suffused the girl's skin from head to toe, but she didn't run or pull away. Was she truly here willingly? Who would do such a thing for their first time? Bad enough to let a stranger take her innocence, but then keep her for a week? That seemed cruel.

"Now, where shall we start the bidding? I think two thousand pounds."

"Two thousand!" someone in the crowd shouted.

Jasper edged closer. "Why do I feel as if I recognize her?"

That feeling returned, the one that told Lucien the answer was staring him right in the face, like a maths problem he couldn't solve. He scowled as the bidding progressed, now above eight thousand pounds. "I feel as though I do, too. Who—?"

All of a sudden Lucien's body jerked. The puzzle clicked into place, the solution as plain as dirt. That golden hair and those big round eyes that used to stare at him like he was the most fascinating man on earth.

No. *No, no, no.*

Lady E. *Eliza.*

"No," he repeated. "I don't believe it."

"Who?"

"Goddamn it. Robert's sister. Lady Eliza." Her brother had been the Earl of Barnett before he died.

Sharp pain pushed under Lucien's sternum, the familiar guilt twisting him up inside. The memories rushed through him, of the three of them—Jasper, Robert and Lucien—and their steadfast friendship. Without siblings of his own, Lucien had considered the two men like brothers, and he'd spent quite a bit of time at Robert's home. That was back when everything was simpler. Back when Lucien actually gave a damn about being a duke and doing right by his responsibilities.

He remembered Eliza. She'd been a serious girl with a keen head for numbers, and Lucien used to give her maths problems to solve at the dinner table. Robert had tried to quiet her, saying it wasn't appropriate for a girl, but Lucien enjoyed the interactions with her. There had been something pure and innocent about her, a thirst for knowledge so sharp he could almost touch it.

The last time he saw her was at Robert's funeral, a sad-eyed fourteen-year-old girl gripping the hand of her younger sister. The two girls had been surrounded by family—or at least what he'd assumed to be family.

So why was she here, selling her body to a stranger?

"Fuck," Jasper said. "We have to help her, Luc—and I don't have the funds left to outbid them."

Eliza bit her lip and ducked her head, holding onto the auctioneer as if her legs wouldn't hold her without support. What had brought Robert's sister here, nothing more than skin and bones, willing to sell her innocence to the highest bidder? Where was her second cousin, the current earl? Why wasn't she married, with a husband taking care of her?

Robert wouldn't want this for her.

Rathbone called out a bid for fifteen thousand pounds, an outrageous sum of money.

Before Lucien could blink, the words tumbled out of his mouth. "Twenty thousand pounds."

"Twenty-five." Rathbone's voice cut through the room, his lifeless eyes daring Lucien to outbid him.

Undeterred, Lucien glared at the other man. "Thirty."

Rathbone's mouth flattened, frustration and determination etched in every line of his face. "Thirty-two."

The idea of Rathbone winning Eliza and subjecting her to his . . .proclivities sent a cold streak of fear through Lucien. He would not allow it to happen. He'd wager his entire estate, his fortune, his *life* to prevent it.

Tossing back the rest of his drink, he slammed the glass on the table. "We all have things to do, so I will cease wasting everyone's time. Fifty thousand pounds."

CHAPTER 2

No one spoke. The man with the lower bid stood up and stormed out, which meant the auction was now over.

She'd been sold.

Eliza clutched the arm of the auctioneer like a safety line, her lungs sucking in air. Was this truly happening?

"Fifty thousand pounds, it is! Lady E is sold to that gentleman there for the next seven nights."

The room broke out in applause, and Eliza's mind reeled at the staggering amount as she was led off stage.

It was . . .unthinkable. With this amount of money, she could take Fanny to a sanitarium in America with fresh air and healing waters. They could buy a nice house somewhere no one knew them and start over. She could finally attend a university.

Once upon a time, she'd hoped to study at one of the women's colleges at Oxford. Her brother laughed at this, saying an earl's daughter needn't be well educated. They'd fought over it many times, with Robert insisting aristocratic ladies should marry and reproduce, not attend college. Eliza held onto that dream, however, planning to prove him wrong.

"Good for you, dearie!" one of the women cheered in the anteroom as Eliza entered.

"I'm a virgin, too, if it could get me fifty thousand quid," another one said.

"Cor, you ain't no virgin, Jane," came a shout. "Your cunt's been ridden more than a horse."

Eliza was shown to a separate room to wait. Within seconds, the door opened and Eliza crossed her arms over her chest in an attempt at modesty. Probably pointless, but it bolstered her courage.

Two men entered. The larger man was the club's owner—and the other was the masked man who'd bought her. He was tall and fit, and younger than she'd anticipated.

The owner closed the door. "Lady E, I'd like to present you with your buyer."

The bidder reached up and untied his mask. When it fell, Eliza gasped, her body rocking as if she'd been dealt a blow.

No, impossible. Utterly impossible.

Blackwood.

More specifically, Lucien, the Duke of Blackwood. Her late brother's best friend.

And Eliza's girlhood obsession.

Oh, God. Every bit of her skin burned as if she stood too close to a fire. Lucien had bid on her. Had paid fifty thousand pounds to bed her and take her virginity. Was she dreaming right now?

Emotions fluttered in her chest, and any embarrassment over appearing half-naked in a room full of men was replaced with relief. It wasn't a stranger who would take her virginity.

Instead, it was a man she'd known as a girl—the serious and kind duke who gave her maths problems to solve at the dinner table, much to the chagrin of her older brother. The man who caused a buzzing sensation under her skin every time she looked at him.

Yes, Lucien was exactly the right man for her first time.

The owner spoke first. "You have any troubles, you come to me, miss," he said, jerking a thumb to his chest. "These gents know what happens if they misbehave."

"Leave us," Blackwood said to the other man, his eyes never leaving Eliza's face. "And I'll have a word with you later about some of the *gents* you allow to participate in these proceedings."

After a frown in the duke's direction, the owner left them alone, and Eliza could feel her heart pounding in her chest as she regarded him. He was so . . .much. Still handsome, with his same windswept black hair and intense brown-green eyes, but his features had sharpened in the last five years. His shoulders had widened, too. Blimey, he was attractive.

"Thank goodness it's you," Eliza blurted. "I was worried about who would buy me."

"I'm certainly surprised, as well. Care to explain?"

He spoke to her as if she were a child who needed reprimanding, which she didn't like, nor did she understand. "What needs explaining, Your Grace? It's a fairly straightforward exchange. I have something to offer and Your Grace has purchased it."

Lucien cocked a brow. "Straightforward? Tonight was anything but, Lady Eliza."

"Please don't call me that." No one used her honorific any longer.

"Why? You are a lady."

"I *was* a lady. That was a long time ago, Your Grace."

"I'll stop calling you a lady if you stop calling me Your Grace. Now, where is your family?"

"Dead, except for my sister."

He winced. "I meant your brother's successor. The new earl."

"Haven't a clue. He turned Fanny and I out five years ago."

Lucien's jaw fell open. "He . . .turned you out? Without providing for you at all?"

This was old news, so Eliza lifted a shoulder. "Apparently Robert hadn't altered his will to include us. Everything went to William, his second cousin."

"Your cousin let it be known you'd gone to live with an aunt in Scotland."

"I have no aunt in Scotland."

"Dash it," he muttered, pinching the bridge of his nose between a thumb and forefinger. "Why not hire a solicitor to look into the matter, then?"

"With what funds, Your Grace?"

"Then why not come to me? Or to Jasper? We gladly would have helped you."

It hadn't occurred to Eliza to beg from Robert's friends, not while she was focused on finding food and shelter. Besides, no one had reached out after the funeral. Every friend and acquaintance forgot about her and Fanny, just two more young girls who were someone else's problem.

Which meant they were no one's problem.

Regardless, she had no choice but to cope with their situation and do it quickly. And, Eliza didn't mind bragging, she'd done a damn decent job of providing for the two of them. If not for Fanny's illness, they would gladly have lived out their days in their rented one-room apartment in Shoreditch. The aristocracy, Eliza discovered, weren't as essential as they believed. Happiness could be found outside of Mayfair.

In fact, being common was generally a relief. The life she'd once lived, with its restrictions and excess and expectations, had been entirely at a man's whim—first her father, then her brother. And even that had all been taken away by another man, her cousin.

She and Fanny lived simpler lives now, but lives of their own choosing, with no one controlling them. Eliza would never allow a man to dictate her future again.

Which was why she would make good on this transaction. An even exchange: her virginity for fifty thousand pounds. Her decision, her control.

Lucien stood, shrugged out of his coat, then came to drape it over her shoulders. The fine wool caressed her bare skin, while the smell of cigar and sandalwood filled her head. She could still feel the warmth from his body on the material, and it sank into her bones. "Thank you," she said gratefully.

"Eliza, honestly. Why didn't you come to me? You look malnourished. I fear a strong wind will blow you over."

That stung. She frowned up at him. "We're doing fine for ourselves. If not for Fanny's—" She snapped her jaw closed. Her sister's illness was not anyone's business.

"Fanny's what?"

"Nothing."

Simple transaction, even exchange. Then she and Fanny would start over in America.

She lifted her chin and gave him what she hoped was an eager smile. "So, when do our seven nights begin?"

* * *

LUCIEN FROWNED, irritated she'd even ask. "Never."

She gaped, her eyes revealing her surprise and confusion, so he held up a hand and said, "However, I will give you the fifty thousand pounds."

"Why on earth would you do that?"

"Because your brother was a friend of mine." His best friend, actually. *And I'm responsible for his death.*

The furrow between her brows deepened. "You cannot give me the money outright."

The words hung there, but he couldn't make sense of them. She was *protesting*? Why wasn't she relieved? She couldn't *want* to sleep with him; she'd sold her innocence for coin. "Why not?"

"Because I would feel beholden to you."

Beholden? She deserved this money. Had Robert known, he would've enlisted Lucien's promise to take care of his sisters. Then she never would've ended up in this predicament—too thin and selling her body like a common streetwalker.

"You won't take my money, but it's fine to sell your virginity to the highest bidder? To a stranger? Come, Eliza. Be sensible. Let's put this ugliness behind us, and I'll ensure that you and Fanny have all the money you ever need."

"Why?"

"Because your brother was my closest friend."

"Still, that is no reason to give me a huge sum of money for nothing."

"It's what your brother would have wanted."

"I don't understand. You didn't bid on me because you wanted to sleep with me? You don't wish to take my virginity?"

Did she sound disappointed, or was he imagining it? A whisper of heat snaked along his spine, but shame quickly followed. While he was a dissolute bastard, he hadn't ever taken advantage of a woman—and he wouldn't start with the little sister of his dead best friend. "Absolutely not. Your brother would be horrified."

"My brother is dead. I no longer have the luxury of wondering over his feelings—not when there are far more pressing matters at hand."

"Regardless, I won't f—" He stopped himself from using the crude word, which was definitely not appropriate to say in front of a lady. "I won't sleep with you."

"Why did you bid on me, then, if you didn't fancy sleeping with me?"

"To save you from the jackals out there. I know those men, and none of them are worthy of you." *Including me.*

"If you won't sleep with me, I'll just arrange for another auction."

The back of his neck grew hot. "Absolutely not. You'll take my money and go live your life."

"No, I won't. I won't take money for nothing. Never does a woman any good."

He could hear a hint of the East End in her speech, and his guilt doubled, sharpening his tone. "I'll not allow you to enter another auction. The owner wouldn't dare risk my ire."

"This is ridiculous. Am I so hideous, then?"

Guilt slashed his insides at her words. "That isn't it at all. You're quite lovely, if I am being honest."

An understatement, actually. Eliza was glorious, even more so up close, with lush blonde hair barely contained by pins, and blue eyes that were almost aqua, like the Mediterranean Sea in the morning.

Her body was too thin, but she had womanly curves that any man would appreciate—and soon those curves would fill out.

Lucien would personally see to it. From now on, Robert's sisters would want for nothing. By next week, they'd be nibbling on tea cakes and petit fours in a drawing room somewhere, doted on by a collection of servants. Everything would be set to rights.

He couldn't bring Robert back, but he could see to Eliza's future.

Her nose wrinkled adorably as she studied him. "Then why not take my virginity? If there's a woman in your bed at the moment, I'm certain she'll understand."

"It's *women*, actually, and that hardly matters. I won't bed you."

"Even when you've paid for it?"

"When she is the little sister of my best friend, the answer remains no."

She wrapped his coat tighter around her body as she stood. "My brother is gone. You cannot continue to use him as a reason. It's illogical."

"You'll accept the money, Eliza. Save your innocence for a husband."

"No. I won't accept the money until you've had your seven nights. It's a fair exchange, and I'd rather have you than some other titled lord who won't care if he hurts me or not."

I'd rather have you.

Oh, Christ. He couldn't. It was wrong to even consider it, despite the dark thrill those words gave him.

Ready to put an end to the discussion, he stalked forward until he loomed over her. "You'll take the money, Eliza. No bedding and no seven nights. Stop being childish. Now, come. I'll see you home."

Her eyes flashed fire as she took a step back. "I'm not a child, and I'm able to see myself home."

"In this city? At this hour? Dressed like that? Absolutely not."

"I have clothes here. I'm used to doing for myself, Your Grace."

"Stop calling me that—and I will see you home if I have to tie your hands and feet and carry you out of here like a rolled-up carpet. Believe me, no one would stop me."

"Fine," she said, taking off his coat and shoving it at him. "At the very least it'll save me the fare."

Relieved, he requested her clothing, then waited outside the door while Eliza dressed. When she emerged, she was wearing a shabby brown garment hanging loose on her too-thin frame. He took her hand, not giving her a chance to escape. "My carriage is out front."

They didn't speak on the way. He could sense her unhappiness, but he didn't care. She would learn how this was going to go. He would give her the money and a house, a new life for her and Fanny, and she would accept it.

Then perhaps his guilt would ease a tiny fraction and he'd be able to sleep at night.

When he jerked open the carriage door, movement inside startled him. Oh, bollocks. How had he forgotten about Mollie and Ginny?

"Your Grace," Mollie said, wide-eyed as she took in the young girl at his side. "You said you weren't buying one tonight."

"I didn't. Move over, loves."

Mollie and Ginny slid to the far side of the carriage, sitting across from each other. From their swollen lips and disheveled clothes, it was clear his mistresses had been busy whilst he'd been away, but he was too worried about Robert's sister to regret missing the fun. He assisted Eliza inside then followed. The four of them barely fit, their knees bumping into one another, but it couldn't be helped.

"Where to, Eliza?"

"Kingsland Road in Shoreditch, please."

After he relayed the direction to his driver an awkward silence fell inside the carriage. He was about to make introductions when Eliza turned to the girls and blurted, "Hello, I'm Eliza. The duke bought my virginity tonight. We're going to spend the next seven nights together."

Before Lucien could correct that statement, Mollie dropped her hand on Lucien's thigh, close to his groin. "Is that what you want, darling? A little bit of blood and trepidation? Ginny and I can accommodate you."

"I'm not taking her virginity. Eliza is the sister of a friend of mine. We are seeing her home."

Eliza waved her hand. "He's still a bit overwhelmed at the prospect. Never fear, I'll bring him around. Actually, perhaps you ladies can help me. What are the duke's preferences in bed?"

Ginny and Mollie grinned, eyes sparkling like they'd made a new friend, while Lucien scowled. Just as Ginny opened her mouth to speak, Lucien pointed at her. "Do not answer that." Then he pinned Eliza with a hard stare, one he rarely used anymore. "Eliza, stop it this instant. We will not sleep together."

She turned to the street, ignoring him. Something told him she hadn't quite agreed, but he would convince her. He was quite in control of his cock, thank you very much, and it had no chance of meeting Eliza's quim. Ever.

Eventually they pulled up to a sad-looking East End building, and Lucien's blood turned cold. Fucking hell, it was terrible. Garbage littered the street and there was clearly a stable close by. Drunken men loitered on the stoop two houses down.

Robert's sisters lived here?

"Absolutely not," he snapped, watching a rat scurry into an alley. "Pack your things, Eliza. I'm taking you and Fanny back to Mayfair."

The girl had the audacity to reach for the handle like he hadn't spoken. "You cannot order me around, Your Grace."

"My fifty thousand pounds says I can, actually. Hurry up. We'll wait."

Her eyes narrowed as she jabbed a finger in his direction. "I *knew* it. I knew you would use that money to try to lord over my life—which is why this must remain a simple business transaction. You are not buying *me*; you are buying my body for seven nights. There is a difference."

Frustrated, he adjusted his tone to plead with her. "I cannot in good conscience leave you here in this neighborhood one second longer. My God, Eliza. You had such big plans when you were younger—you even talked of going to university. This is not the life you wanted. Go, pack your things. You're coming to stay with me in Grosvenor Square."

Mouths agape, Ginny and Mollie were following the conversation, heads swiveling as if they were at a lawn tennis match. He remained focused on Robert's maddening sister, who was currently staring at him like he was muck under her shoe.

"No," she said, her voice brittle and angry. "I've built a life here. It may not meet with Your Grace's approval, but it's ours—and no man will ever take it away from us. I'll see you tomorrow night."

She threw open the door and slipped out of the carriage before he could stop her. Damn it.

Once on the ground, she hurried away, but Lucien unfolded from the vehicle and gave chase. Unfortunately, he lost her in the dark, crooked streets almost immediately. "Christ!" he yelled, kicking an empty jar with his boot as he trudged back to his carriage.

Tomorrow, he would find Eliza and her sister, even if he had to tear the whole city apart to do it.

CHAPTER 3

His bed was enormous.

Eliza stood in Lucien's empty bedroom with just the silvery light of the moon to guide her. She and Fanny discussed this plan many times today. They decided the quickest way to get the money was for Eliza to show up and seduce him. Then their seven nights would commence, and he would have no choice but to see it through.

A monetary gift, even from Lucien, was too risky. As she'd seen many times, gifts from men always came with strings. Like when a former landlord agreed to give them a few more days on their rent—if Eliza showed him her quim. She'd refused and moved them out the next day.

Then there was the first doctor to see Fanny, who offered free treatment if Eliza rubbed her stocking feet on his crotch after every visit. Most recently was the owner of a garment factory who agreed to help Eliza move up to a better paying position, but only if she became his mistress.

Did anyone honestly believe Lucien would give her that much money, wish her well, and disappear from her life? She snorted in the darkness. Even last night he'd tried ordering her about—using just the *promise* of the money as leverage. Eliza wouldn't let another man control her or her sister again.

This time was *her* choice. She wanted to earn this money, fair and square.

Her gaze drifted back to the bed, and her corset suddenly felt too tight, her clothes too itchy. The pulse between her legs was distracting, an insistent ache that began whenever she thought of him. Blooming hell, she was looking forward to this.

As a girl, she'd experienced a giddiness in Lucien's presence, like her chest was full of butterflies and bees. She stared at him during his visits, obsessed with his soft smile and biting sense of humor. They both liked maths and playing croquet, and what more had a young girl needed to know other than that? He was utterly perfect to her mind.

So, where was he? Would he stay out the entire night? Pleasuring two mistresses was double the work, after all. Would he have the verve to relieve Eliza of her innocence tonight?

His exhaustion would definitely add a wrinkle to her plan, but it wouldn't dissuade her. She could wait and return tomorrow night. And the night after that. As many nights as it took to convince him to take her virginity. It had to work eventually.

Footsteps in the corridor caught her attention. She slipped into the shadows, held her breath, and waited. It could be Lucien—or a servant. And Eliza hadn't crossed the city in the dead of night, crawled through an unlocked window, and crept through his house . . . only to be thrown out by a snooty valet.

The latch turned and a large shape filled the doorway.

Lucien.

She bit her lip, her body vibrating with . . . nerves. Excitement. Fear. More excitement. Surely there were other emotions, but she couldn't pinpoint them.

He closed the door and draped the room in darkness once more. Her eyes had already adjusted, so she could see him rip off his top coat, then toe off his shoes. "Fuck me," he growled.

Why was he angry?

Stomping to the bed, he flopped down onto his back. "Bugger it." His broad chest rose and fell with the force of his breath.

When he didn't move, she stepped out of the darkness. "May I help, Your Grace?"

Blinking, he came up on his elbows. "Eliza?"

"Hello, duke."

His brow creased, the lines too numerous to count. "They looked for you all bloody day. Turned Shoreditch upside down. I've been going out of my mind with worry ever since last night."

He'd tried to find her? She didn't know whether to be flattered or horrified. "I told you I would come tonight."

"Excellent. I'll write you a bank draft and send you back home."

"Let me undress first. How would you like to take my virginity? With me on my back, or on my hands and knees? I did see a drawing once of a woman upside down—"

"Eliza," he snapped. "None of that is happening. I cannot sleep with you."

Oh. He'd already exhausted himself, then. "Have your mistresses worn you out tonight?"

"Jesus, no—and do not think for one second that I have issues with stamina. I meant I cannot sleep with you and live with myself. It isn't right."

She smothered a smile. Poor man. He had no idea who he was up against. The last five years had taught Eliza patience. She knew that with slow and steady progress, she would eventually reach any goal she set.

And her current goal was for Lucien to want her desperately enough to overlook his sense of misplaced honor toward her dead brother.

She moved closer to the bed and ran her fingers over his shin bone. "You could kiss me. That wouldn't be so terrible, would it?"

The noise that escaped his throat sounded tortured. "I know what you are doing, you clever girl. You are hoping I'll kiss you and become so overcome with lust that I end up between your thighs."

He wasn't that far off. "Actually, I was hoping you would show me what a real kiss feels like. The kisses I've experienced have—"

"Who has kissed you?" Abruptly, he sat up, his dark eyes blazing. "Were they rough with you? Did they force you? Because I swear to God..."

"Calm down, Lucien." She rose and moved between his legs. They were face-to-face now, her hands coming to rest on his shoulders. "They were mere boys, sloppy and inexperienced. No one forced me. I kissed them because I wanted to, just like I want to kiss you."

Seconds ticked by while he examined her face, brow wrinkled like he couldn't believe she actually wanted to kiss him. Yet she did. Badly.

She liked this serious, protective side of him, more like the Lucien she remembered, the one who had defended her intelligence to Robert and her parents. The man who made her feel valued and *seen* at a time when young girls were often ignored and dismissed. Lord, how she'd loved him once.

Finally, his mouth hitched in a way that caused her stomach to flip. "I am definitely no sloppy and inexperienced boy."

"No, you certainly are not, which is why I want to know what it's like to be kissed by you."

He leaned in, as if drawn to her, but didn't come close enough to actually kiss her. His breath ghosted over her skin as he spoke. "I would make it so good for you. I would take my time, explore every bit of you with my lips and tongue. You would feel so safe with me, angel. I'd never let anyone hurt you again."

Was he talking about kissing...or something more?

Her lower body clenched at his seductive words, the area between her legs growing damp and hot. It would be so easy to believe him, so easy to let herself rely on someone else to take care of her. But she would not trade her hard-fought independence for anything. Lucien could have her body for seven nights, but he would never have more.

She said none of this, however. She merely edged forward until their lips nearly touched. "Show me, Lucien. *Please.*"

* * *

LUCIEN'S HEAD SWAM—AND the dizziness had nothing to do with the scotch he'd swallowed earlier. No, his little angel had him off-balance, sneaking into his bedroom and asking him to kiss her. God, he wanted to. More than anything else, he longed to drag her beneath him and show her how good it could be between them. Teach her how to please him.

I could be her first.

Fuck. He had to stop thinking like that.

As much as he wanted to watch as his cock speared her virgin flesh, he couldn't. This was Robert's sister, a proper lady, and she would hate him if she knew the truth behind her brother's death. That Lucien was the reason for the loss of her family home, her wealth and position.

So despite his desire for her, it was dangerous to contemplate fucking her—and she deserved better.

Moonlight bathed her in a soft glow, showing off her slightly parted lips and the flush on her cheeks. She was absolutely lovely, her face free of cosmetics and lip paint. He stared at the delicate curve of her jaw, the slim column of her throat, both begging to be explored by his mouth. Was the skin there as soft as it appeared?

No, no, no. He couldn't.

Could he?

Her fingers found their way into his hair, their bodies nearly flush, with her lower half appallingly close to his. He wanted to touch her so badly, his hands shook with it. Why wasn't she afraid? Weren't most virgins supposed to be terrified, wilting creatures?

Eliza appeared almost . . . aroused.

Was that possible?

"Why aren't you scared?" he whispered, their breath mingling.

"Because it's you."

Swallowing, he came to a decision right then. As long as he didn't fuck her, he could show her everything her curious little heart desired —and in the meantime convince her to stay here until he could get her into better lodgings.

He was not above using pleasure to achieve what he wanted, and he wanted Robert's sisters safe and back where they belonged in a decent neighborhood.

"I'm going to kiss you, Eliza."

Her response was instant. "All right."

"But just kissing." He could do this. Just a few minutes exploring her mouth, rubbing her sweet little tongue with his, before he made her agree to return to Mayfair. "Do you remember when we used to do maths together?"

"Yes, of course." The words came out on a soft sigh, as if the memory was a good one. He hoped so—those were pleasant memories for him, too. Clever and eager, she kept up with his complex questions, and he'd been suitably impressed.

"Kissing is like solving an equation," he told her, sliding his hands onto her hips. "You have this mystery to unravel, a puzzle, and it requires careful examination and thought. Planning and patience. The answer is there, but you cannot rush it."

"And what is the answer?"

"For me, it's discovering what makes a woman purr into my mouth and rub against me like she longs to feel me everywhere. What makes her hot and eager, wet between her legs."

He paused, half-hoping he'd shocked or scared her into leaving. It was best for both of them if this never went any further.

"But I already feel that," she said, "and you haven't even kissed me yet."

His cock pulsed, a jolt of lust careening through him at her honesty, and he moved closer. "Then just relax. Let me taste you."

A willing pupil, she held perfectly still, allowing him to close the distance and cover her mouth with his. He briefly wondered how far she'd gone with those boys, whether she'd let any of them stroke her between her thighs, but he shoved those thoughts away. Tonight was just kissing.

Her lips were soft and wet, like she'd licked them in preparation for his kiss, and he moved carefully, gently, learning the shape and feel of her, while giving her the chance to do the same. He swept back and forth lightly, brushing and teasing, enjoying the anticipation building between them. Many partners complained kissing was unnecessary, but Lucien loved it. There was something about the connection, the shared breath and slick exchange of saliva, that was both dirty and beautiful. Hedonistic and necessary.

That he was kissing this particular woman, the one who used to look at him with stars in her eyes, made it all the sweeter. He suddenly remembered how her stare made him feel twenty feet tall all those years ago, like he was the only man in the room. How had he ever forgotten?

Desperate for more, he deepened the kiss, holding her face in his palms and adding more pressure. Then he nipped her lips, and was rewarded when her mouth parted to allow him inside.

It was worth the wait.

Her tongue was wet and hot, and he suddenly couldn't get enough. She was thorough, her mouth mimicking his movements, and he lost himself in the flicks and swirls, the moans and gasps as the kiss wore on. Part of him worried this might be a mistake, because he liked it *too much*, but the other part—the selfish and depraved half—wanted to take everything she offered and ruin her for other men.

Ruin her, period.

This is Eliza, Robert's sister. Get a hold of yourself, man.

Somehow he managed to hold himself in check, not once losing the thin threads of his self control. When her hands gripped his shoulders, he fought the urge to move closer. When her fingers slid into his hair, he fought the urge to cup her breasts in his palms.

And when she shifted into the cradle of his thighs, he fought the urge to grind his cock into her mound.

It wasn't easy, especially when her eagerness and innocence beckoned him like a treat just out of reach. But this must remain a kiss, nothing more.

So when she shoved his shoulders, he wasn't ready for it. Actually, he had no idea what was happening until he was flat on his back on the bed. "Eliza, what—"

His jaw snapped shut when she crawled over him, her legs straddling his thighs. Oh, Christ. What was happening?

The ceiling stared down at him blankly, as if to mock him. *You fool. Your hubris knows no bounds.*

Weakly, he tried to move but it was too late. Her glorious weight came down on him and his hands clasped the back of her knees under her skirts. Before he could order her to get up, she rocked her core over his erection, and white-hot pleasure shot through him like a bolt of electricity, obliterating everything else.

Goddamn it. Need clawed inside his belly, robbing him of all good sense. Why was fate so fucking cruel?

She pulled a small tin from her dress pocket. "I brought a shield."

He stared at her hand, his cock throbbing. The idea that she'd come prepared, that she'd turned aggressive—that she *wanted* this so desperately—nearly did him in. It would be so easy to free his erection and let her slide down, pierce her virgin cunt slowly. She would undoubtedly grip him tightly, tighter than anything he'd ever—

No. This wasn't right.

Eliza was a lady, whether she admitted it or not. Gently bred and raised to expect marriage. Lucien couldn't treat her like a mistress, no matter the fever currently burning inside him to have her. She deserved better.

Carefully, he moved her off him and onto the bed. "Let's slow down, shall we? There's no rush."

"What are you talking about? Of course, there is a bleeding rush. This is only seven nights, Lucien."

"I've always loved the sound of my name coming out of your mouth." It was an idiotic thing to say, but absolutely true.

Her mouth curved in a way that almost made him nervous, as if he'd handed her a dangerous weapon. "Indeed, 'tis a nice name." She leaned over him, her hand firmly on his chest. "Will you kiss me again, Lucien?"

"No, because you and your shield are attempting to turn this into a deflowering, and I most definitely need you to stay flowered."

"That is not a word," she said with a smile.

"Perhaps, but you know what I mean. I will not bed you."

"You may use crude words with me, you know. I promise you

won't offend my delicate sensibilities. I told you, I'm no longer a lady, and I've heard all manner of improper words in the last five years."

"You are a lady and you shouldn't know those words."

"Like fuck?"

"Dash it, Eliza. This has gone far enough—"

"Fine." She held the shield up where he could see it and slowly placed the tin on the small table by his bed. "There. Now we may focus on kissing and whatever else may happen."

He groaned as images of *whatever else* raced through his mind. "You don't know what you're asking for."

"Why? What are you worried might happen?"

"Any number of wicked scenarios that involve your naked body."

"Such as?"

"Things I'll never share with you."

"Because you're not attracted to me?"

"Because of *Robert*," he snapped. "Have you not been paying attention, woman?"

"Right." Her lips twitched like she was amused. "What if we focused on wicked scenarios that involved your naked body instead?"

While his cock was more than eager for this plan, Lucien wasn't fooled. She didn't know the first thing about pleasuring a man. How could she, as a virgin?

It was past time to illuminate her innocence and their incompatibility. If this was the only way to do it, so be it. Then she would see this was foolish, that she wasn't ready for seven nights of sin with a virtual stranger. That she should save herself for a husband.

Whether she wanted to admit it or not, she was a lady. No doubt she'd go running from the room the moment his cock appeared.

Indeed, this was the best way to put an end to this right now.

Stretching his arms up above his head, he spread his body out like a buffet, a feast for the taking. "If you can ask nicely for it, then maybe I'll let you."

CHAPTER 4

Was this a new game? If so, Eliza was ready. It was no hardship to explore him. Attractive and well proportioned, the duke was big, his clothes outlining a fit frame with a broad chest and flat stomach. A light dusting of whiskers coated his jaw, and she longed to test the roughness of that skin with her fingertips.

"May I touch you?"

One of his dark eyebrows lifted. "I'm no thirteen-year-old boy, Eliza. If you wish to touch me, you need to be explicit. Tell me where and what you plan to do."

She bit the inside of her cheek to keep from smiling. Was he being deliberately cruel to embarrass her? Probably. Lucien was very clever —probably the smartest man she'd ever met—and fixated on his loyalty to Robert. No doubt he was hoping she would blush and stammer, as any gently bred virgin would in this situation.

But Eliza was not the same gently bred girl, not anymore.

Drawing closer, she ran a fingertip over his stomach. "May I unfasten your trousers, Your Grace?"

"And why would you like to unfasten my trousers, angel?"

In for a penny, as the saying went.

"To see your cock. I want to lavish it with kisses and lick it all over."

Lucien's face paled, his lips parting ever so slightly. He seemed to be stuck, not breathing, his gaze fixated on her mouth. Was he imagining what it would feel like?

"How . . .?" His voice trailed off.

"Had you thought I was unfamiliar with the act? Or, too embarrassed to speak about it?" She shook her head. "I'm not the sheltered girl you once knew."

"Have you ever . . .done that before?"

"No, but I'd like for you to teach me how."

His eyes slammed closed, his face twisted as if he were in pain. "Jesus, Eliza. You shouldn't say such things to a man like me."

"And what type of man are you?"

"A degenerate. A selfish wastrel. A man who will ride you so hard, you'll feel it for days to come."

Gorblimey.

An inferno ignited in her belly, followed by waves of wanting that skimmed through her veins. Was he hoping to scare her? Because honestly, the idea of his big muscled body moving over hers, giving pleasure that would haunt her long after, was more than appealing. It reinforced her sense that Lucien was the perfect man to rid her of her virginity.

He would take care with her. Provide her with seven nights of fun, then she would depart for America—and he would return to his mistresses and ducal debauchery.

She gave him her best attempt at a sultry smile. "If that was intended to deter me, dear man, I'm afraid you have failed."

He groaned, his hands scrubbing his face. "Has anyone ever told you that you are stubborn?"

"Many times." Fanny mentioned it quite often. But Eliza preferred *determined*, a trait that had helped her and her sister survive after being tossed out like trash. "Which means your resistance is futile."

He pinned her with his brownish-green stare. "Let's make a bargain."

She never agreed to anything without hearing all the details. Being cheated once in the Covent Garden market had taught her that. "Tell me the terms first."

"You let me pleasure you tonight. My trousers stay on. Then you and Fanny move in here tomorrow, and we discuss setting up a new life for you both."

"No. Here are my terms: you teach me how to pleasure you tonight, then I will return tomorrow night for more lessons."

"Damn it, Eliza."

He started to sit up—probably to throw her out or yell at her—and she panicked. Moving swiftly, she threw her leg over his hips and moved on top of him. Again. But this time her core landed on his erection, which was thick and hard under her center. They both froze.

This was his cock. Directly between her legs. Good God. It was much larger than she'd expected.

"What are you doing?" His voice sounded strangled.

She hadn't the faintest. "I'm not certain but it feels right. Should I move off you?"

"No. Yes. Wait, no."

His hesitation was promising. Because begging worked earlier for kissing, she tried it again. "Teach me, Lucien." She splayed her fingers on his chest and rocked her hips. Sakes alive, that felt delicious. "Please."

When she did it once more, they both groaned.

"Christ," he murmured as he fell back onto the bed. "I'm definitely going to Hell for even considering this."

"Is that a yes?"

"Eliza, let me lick you—"

She rolled her hips along the large ridge again and shivered as pleasure coursed through her. Leaning forward, she whispered, "You bought me, Lucien. You may do whatever you like with me tonight."

His cock jerked against her. Oh, he *liked* that.

She kept going. "Wouldn't you like to be my first?"

"Oh, God," he said on a rough exhale. "Why are you torturing me?"

"Do you want me to stop . . .or do you want to show me what it feels like to have your cock between my legs?"

"Jesus Christ!" He arched, every muscle pulled taut, with his expression twisted in what appeared like agony. Without warning, his hands shot out to clasp her hips. His eyes were wild, a man pushed to the edge of his sanity. "Roll your hips, darling," he rasped. "Make us both come."

"What about your trousers?"

"They remain on. Trust me, you'll like it. Rub your sex over the cloth and along my shaft." He guided her. "Just keep going. Yes, exactly like that."

Tingles raced along the back of her thighs as she dragged her body over his. Why was this so amazing? The friction had her seeing stars. The strength of her reaction surprised her, but she wasn't worried.

Lucien will take care of me.

She knew it in her bones. He'd been so kind to her all those years ago, telling Robert to mind his own business when her brother tried to belittle her. Lucien had made her feel special, and she hadn't forgotten it.

His fingertips tightened on her hips. "How badly do you want to please me, angel?"

She peeked at him through her lashes. "Very, very badly, Your Grace."

"Then we do this once. One time and no more. No seven nights, just this. Our clothes stay on. Say you understand."

He didn't ask if she agreed, only that she understood. Hiding a smile, she kept churning her hips, grinding on top of him. "I understand."

He grunted and let his eyelids fall briefly, his long eyelashes kissing his cheeks. "You will thank me someday."

Doubtful, but there was no arguing with him, not now.

"Does it feel good for you?" Her palms rested on his stomach as she moved, again and again, in a steady rhythm. "Because I think it feels incredible."

"God, yes, it feels good. I'm so hard for you."

The more she rocked, the more the heat built inside her. The pleasure made her dizzy, like she was drunk on sensation, chasing a high slightly out of reach. She dug her nails into his skin, the ache drawing tighter, her body on fire. "Oh, Lucien."

"Yes, keep going." His chest heaved and his lips parted on a ragged breath. "Lift your skirts with one hand. Let me see you drag your pussy over my cock and make yourself come. I need to see it."

Her thighs trembled as she gathered her skirts in her fingers and lifted them out of the way. "You're the first man to ever see it," she whispered. "You could also be the first man to touch it."

"Fuck, fuck, fuck," he chanted, his stare locked on the bare skin revealed by the slit in her drawers. "I want that so badly. I want to finger you and lick you and fuck you."

"I see couples doing those things in the alleys," she told him, closing her eyes and imagining her and Lucien in the open air, where anyone could walk by and watch him taking her from behind. The sparks doubled, quadrupled in her blood, and she moved faster, her hips becoming uncoordinated as the pleasure dragged her under.

A searing swell rushed up from her toes, flooding her, and her core contracted as she quivered and shook. It was better than anything she had imagined. The waves caused her to shudder, the man beneath her the only tether to the ground.

"I can see how wet you are," he growled when she floated back to earth. "May I taste it? Please? Run your finger through your slickness and give me one small taste."

It never occurred to her to refuse. He appeared desperate for her, feverish, like he might be close to his own climax, and she wanted to drive him wild. Dipping her finger into her sex, she coated the digit in her arousal and lifted it to his mouth. "Here."

He sucked her finger past his lips and into his mouth, his tongue swirling over her skin greedily. A groan rumbled in his throat and his eyes nearly rolled back in his head. Did he truly like the taste so much as that?

She leaned in and whispered, "Have you ever tasted a virgin before?"

His hips began bucking, nearly unseating her. "Oh, fuck. I'm—" He stiffened and his back bowed, air heaving in and out of his chest, and his shout filled the room to echo off the walls. The erection beneath her pulsed, the cloth of his trousers growing warm and wet on her skin. His *seed*. Pride filled her at his completion. She'd made him do that. Her, a virgin.

He'd never be able to resist her now.

* * *

LUCIEN MAY HAVE UNDERESTIMATED HER.

His sweet little virgin had a wicked mouth and was eager to please. His new favorite qualities in bed, apparently. That this was Robert's sister was a worry for tomorrow. Right now, she was merely Eliza, the woman who caused him to come in his trousers like a schoolboy.

He hadn't expected her to be so . . .filthy. Or competent. She rode him like a thoroughbred at Ascot, and he'd loved every second of it. The proof was now cooling and sticking to his skin.

When she'd lifted her skirts to her waist, the slit in her drawers revealed her cunt and he'd nearly climaxed right then. Christ, she was gorgeous. Downy hair covered her mound, while the pink lips of her sex glistened with arousal. For him. And the taste? Ambrosia. He wanted to bury his face there, breathe her in, taste her and lick her, and have her come on his tongue over and over until they were exhausted.

Grinning, she slid off him. "That was fun. We should do that again. Tomorrow night, say ten o'clock?"

"No. Now, what time may I expect you and Fanny in the morning?"

Her expression cleared, a wariness returning to her gaze. "I beg your pardon?"

"You and Fanny. Moving in tomorrow. What time?"

"We're not moving in with you. I told you this already."

He exhaled heavily. "Eliza, you agreed."

"No, I certainly did not."

"Let me put this plainly. If you and Fanny are not here by nine o'clock tomorrow morning, baggage in hand, there will be no fifty thousand pounds."

"Stop trying to control me with money. And!" She pointed to his crotch. "At the very least you owe me seven thousand one-hundred and forty-two quid."

"And eighty-six pence." Yes, he could do maths, too. "That amount was for your virginity, Eliza, which you still possess."

"This is ridiculous."

"No, ridiculous is you insisting on living in a hovel when I have offered to put you up here."

Her lip curled in distaste, eyes turning cold, but he had no idea how he'd offended her. Every word was the truth.

He kept going, playing his only card. "You may say farewell to the fifty thousand pounds if you do not bring your sister here in the morning."

They stared at one another for a long moment. He could see her mind working, as it had all those years ago at the dinner table when she examined a problem from every side. Logically, as he would. There was no way out of this, though, because he would not bend. She would leave that rat-infested neighborhood and come stay with him, where he would look after her like a ward.

A ward who had once ridden his cock and made them both come.

His chest ached, perhaps with regret. Or perhaps with the knowledge this evening could never be repeated. It didn't matter. He would not take advantage of her whilst she was living under his roof. She needed to feel safe here, well provided for. Exactly as her brother would have expected.

When she didn't speak, he added, "I am merely looking out for you. It's what your brother would have wanted." *And what my guilt demands.*

She gestured to the bed. "Do you sincerely believe if I moved in that *this* would not happen again?"

He felt a real flash of fear in his belly. Eliza dressing and undressing under his roof. Seeing her smile every place he turned.

Watching her eat and laugh over dinner. Thinking about her lying in bed, perhaps touching herself at the memories....

Could he stand it?

He bolted off the bed. Damn it, his trousers were a bloody mess. "I will behave myself," he said with more certainty than he felt. "I trust you can do the same whilst here. Now, I will clean up and see you home. Wait here a few moments."

"That isn't necessary."

"Of course, it is. I'll not have you running pell-mell through the streets of London at this hour."

She studied him, then leaned back and relaxed on the bed. "Whatever Your Grace wants," she murmured with a small smile twisting the edges of her mouth.

The words nearly caused him to trip as he headed to the washroom. God almighty, he liked her compliance. Too much, actually.

You bought me, Lucien. You may do whatever you like with me tonight.

The dark thrill at that shamed him to his soul. He'd bedded his fair share of women in the last ten years, but never had he experienced such mindless lust at a couple of sentences strung together. Yes, he wanted to own her, to be her first. To teach her and ruin her for all others.

But it was dangerous—not to mention wrong.

He spent a few minutes in the washroom cleaning up as best he could, stripping out of his soiled undergarment and putting his trousers back on. The scent of her soaked the cloth, and if it were up to him the garment would never be sent to the laundry. He'd keep them dirty and stained as a reminder of their night together, of the one time his little virgin vixen teased and tormented him.

Finally, he finished putting himself to rights and returned to his bedroom, ready to see Eliza home.

Except the bed was empty. Nor could he find her anywhere inside the townhouse.

She had disappeared.

CHAPTER 5

*E*liza left her flat the next morning at eight o'clock, as usual. She was due at Mrs. O'Toole's, where she would spend the day mending clothes. It didn't pay much, but it was easy work.

The task would keep her hands and mind occupied, which was a relief after last night. Upon returning home from Lucien's, she'd tossed and turned, both angry and relieved. Sated and frustrated. The dratted man should claim her virginity, give her the money, then let her go on her merry way. Why was he insisting on complicating everything?

Fanny agreed with Eliza that accepting the money from Lucien without services rendered was a mistake. Then her sister minimized her illness, saying they didn't need the money quite as badly as that. Eliza knew better.

They did need the money. Eliza hated hearing his sister cough and struggle to breathe at night, and Fanny couldn't work because employers and coworkers were terrified she had consumption. According to Dr. Humphries, the doctor who treated Fanny, it wasn't consumption and a lengthy stay at a sanitarium should help her completely recover. But such facilities were expensive, and their savings wouldn't begin to touch the cost.

"Eliza," a deep voice suddenly said from close behind her. Too close.

She whirled and drew to a stop. The Marquess of Rathbone stood on the walk, looming over her like a gargoyle. Taking a step back, she shivered and rubbed her arms despite the heat outside. "My lord. Good morning."

Three months ago she apprenticed in Rathbone's garment factory. After recognizing her, he made a point to talk to her each time he visited the floor. She was polite, even though the reminder of her brother and her family stung, while doing her best to deter him. Still, Rathbone lingered more and more, distracting her from the work.

When she requested a sewing machine of her own, the manager said Rathbone made those decisions—even though the marquess hadn't promoted any other apprentice. Eliza suspected his involvement was special to her, which should have sent her packing straight away.

Instead, she foolishly approached him and requested a machine. The marquess turned it into an opportunity to proposition her, during which he asked her to become his mistress. Eliza quit that very day, never even collecting her last paycheck.

"There you go, always so busy," he said. "May I offer you a ride?"

A slick black brougham waited at the curb. The idea of sitting in such a confined space with him turned her stomach. "Thank you, my lord, but I'm fine to walk. It's not far."

"Then allow me to walk with you. It would be a shame if you were set upon. These streets are not safe for a young girl like yourself."

"Your lordship is very kind, but that's unnecessary. Good day, sir."

When she started to turn away, he took her arm. He wasn't hurting her, and to a passerby it would appear he was assisting her, but he hadn't asked permission to touch her. If he had, she certainly would not have granted it.

He began leading her along the walk. "See, isn't that better?"

"Please, my lord. Let me go."

"Nonsense. I'm happy to help." He leaned in, his hot breath hitting her skin. "In fact, I know just the sort of help you need. Do not be too proud to accept it from me, girl."

"Rathbone." The word cut through the noise on the street like the crack of a whip.

Lucien was there, the brim of his bowler doing little to hide the absolute fury in his gaze. "I believe the lady asked you to let her go."

Rathbone frowned, but otherwise didn't move. "This doesn't concern you, Blackwood."

"It does, actually. The lady is due with me this morning."

Eliza couldn't believe this. What was Lucien doing here at this hour? How had he found her?

Lucien stared at Rathbone, as if daring him to argue. Tension strung between the two men like a wire, taut and dangerous, and she wondered if they would come to blows.

Using the distraction to her advantage, she pulled free of Rathbone and shifted closer to Lucien. "It's true. His Grace requested my presence today."

A flash of something dark, something terrifying, crossed Rathbone's face before he cleared it. "We will speak later, then." He tipped his bowler and walked in the direction of his carriage.

Lucien took Eliza's arm and began leading her in the opposite direction. She didn't fight him, but she had questions. "What are you doing here? How did you find—"

"Quiet," he snapped.

"Oh, you think to order me about, too?"

"He's watching. Follow me and I'll explain in my carriage."

Glancing over her shoulder, she saw that Rathbone was, in fact, lingering near the street, his hollow eyes tracking her and Lucien as they walked away. A chill slithered over her skin. Unnerved, she pressed her lips together and remained silent.

A block over, a closed black carriage awaited. The conveyance looked totally out of place here, with its shiny lacquered sides and matching horses, and Eliza remembered rides in carriages such as this. She hadn't thought twice about it then, and hadn't realized her privilege until it was taken away by a system and society governed by men.

The reminder annoyed her, so she dug in her heels before Lucien could drag her any closer. "While I'm grateful for your assistance with Rathbone, I'm perilously close to being late for work. So, if you'll excuse me." She tried to tug out of his grasp, but he didn't let go.

"Get in my carriage, Eliza," he growled. "Right now."

Her jaw fell open. "You're angry with me? The bloody nerve! I've done nothing wrong."

He stepped closer and lowered his voice. "Other than sneaking out of my home last night after I told you to wait? Did it ever occur to you that I might be worried sick? That I might have stayed up half the night picturing you eviscerated in some alley?"

She bit the inside of her cheek and shoved aside the guilt. "And I told you I was perfectly fine seeing myself home. As you can see, I was right."

Closing his eyelids tightly like he was struggling for patience, he bit out, "Get in the carriage. You are embarrassing us both, arguing with me like a fishwife on the street."

Anger suffused her entire body. Embarrassing him? This was her neighborhood, not his, and she wouldn't be put back in that restrictive, proper aristocratic box ever again.

She would show him true embarrassment.

Angling back, she shouted, "Corblimey, guv! That's one right big tallywag you 'ave for a toff. Let me get me muff ready and you can roger it proper."

A passerby snickered, and Lucien turned an alarming shade of red. He spoke through clenched teeth. "If you want to see my solicitor, then I suggest you get moving."

She blinked. "Your solicitor? Why?"

"Because I asked him to look into the situation with Robert's estate. Now, do you want to get in on your own, or would you rather I throw you over my shoulder and toss you in myself?"

His solicitor? Hope flared in her chest and she considered whether to go with him. Mrs. O'Toole would understand Eliza's absence, but it meant Eliza wouldn't earn her sixpence for the day.

Perhaps I could earn another seven thousand one-hundred and forty-two quid instead.

Yes, that sounded like a more reasonable financial decision.

Patting Lucien's chest, she smiled. "Whatever Your Grace wishes."

Suspicion crossed his features and his eyes narrowed, yet he said nothing as she climbed inside the fancy carriage. The inside smelled of him—leather and fancy spices—which was a far cry from the ripe horse and refuse odor on the street. She settled into the plush seat and decided to enjoy the day with him.

Soon they set off, the wheels clattering along the uneven Shoreditch streets. They hadn't even gone a block when Lucien growled, "How do you know Rathbone?"

She glanced over at him, wondering at his sharp tone. Was Lucien jealous? No, that was ridiculous. "I worked at his factory for four months."

"He owns a factory?"

"Yes, a garment factory. They make coats and shirts."

"What did you do there?"

"I was an apprentice. Fetched bobbins and learned how to cut and make clothing. I tried to get my own machine, but Rathbone wouldn't allow it unless I granted him certain privileges."

Lucien tensed next to her, his muscles stiff. "That bastard."

"It's not an original story, I'm afraid. Though his offer was better than most. It included a townhouse and a staff of my own."

"I hope you punched him in the jaw."

She lifted a shoulder. "It's not much different from what you offered."

He swung to glare at her, a tinge of red on his high cheekbones. "It's hardly the same. I want to give you fifty thousand pounds and your own home."

"I don't want it, not until the end of our agreement. We have a simple business transaction, Lucien. Nothing more. You cannot order me about or use that money to control me. I am not your ward or your mistress. I am the woman you bought for seven nights."

"My God!" He tossed his bowler onto the opposite seat. "I have never seen such foolishness in all my life. You're wearing threadbare clothing and are clearly in need of a hot meal. You could be wearing diamonds and Worth gowns, woman. Drinking champagne and eating the finest foods, while being waited on by a bevy of servants. Why are you so insistent on clinging to your poverty?"

The words slashed through her, cutting deep. Did he really think so little of her, judging her because she was no longer a spoiled Mayfair princess? Couldn't he see she was something better? She'd been cast out with a sister to take care of, no money, no one to turn to, and had carved out a life for them with her bare hands. With her blood, sweat and tears, and no help from anyone, thank you very much.

And while they might not have a lot, Eliza was proud of every bit of it.

"Nothing comes for free in this life, Your Grace. Not for women. If the past five years have taught me a single thing, it's precisely that."

"You're wrong. I only want to help you as repayment for Robert."

"Repayment? For what?"

He shifted toward the window and fiddled with his cuff. "For ignoring you all this time. For believing that story about Scotland and your aunt and not checking on you myself."

Something about his words didn't ring true. He was lying, but why?

Before she could contemplate what Lucien might be hiding, he lifted her arm and held it. "Did Rathbone hurt you?" he asked quietly, then pressed his warm lips to the sensitive skin inside her wrist.

The shifts in his mood were boggling. Has she ever met a more confusing man? His touch distracted her, though, with his gentle kisses sending goosebumps up and down her arm. "No," she whispered.

"Are you certain?" He lingered there, his warm breath and wet mouth worshipping her skin, and her muscles grew heavy, limbs sinking into the leather. He murmured, "Because I will destroy him and everything he cares about if he ever hurts you."

"Why?"

"Because you're mine, Eliza."

* * *

He hadn't meant to say it.

But once the words were out, Lucien wouldn't take them back. She was his. She'd belonged to him ever since those dinners when they discussed maths and her studies, and when she'd asked him questions about university and his classes. When her insatiable thirst for knowledge had her hanging on his every word, making him feel like the smartest man in the room.

The thought of truly claiming this woman, of being the first to slide inside her body and spill his seed there, had tortured him all night. It had been so long since he felt worthy of such a gift, and he didn't deserve it, especially from Eliza.

She'd hate him if she knew what happened. Only Jasper knew the truth, that Lucien's selfishness had caused Robert's death, and that if Lucien had been there instead . . .

In the end Lucien lost a friend and gained a mountain of guilt.

So, no. He wouldn't fuck her, and he certainly couldn't keep her.

But he could kiss her.

Removing his gloves, he unbuttoned the cuff of her shirtwaist and slid the fabric out of his way. Her skin was soft and supple, and he lavished kisses all the way up her forearm, loving the way she trembled in his grasp. He could still hear her moans in his ears from last night, the sounds of pleasure when she rode his body.

He wanted to hear them again.

She's only allowing this because you bought her.

The lust roaring in his blood cooled. What was he doing? Eliza wasn't his lover or his mistress. Both of them grew carried away last night, lost in the moment, but said moment had passed.

He lowered her arm, rebuttoned her cuff, then set her hand on her lap.

"You are the most confusing man," she said. "For a reprobate, you are surprisingly hard to seduce."

"Is that what you are doing? Trying to seduce me?"

"Yes, you daft man. I still have nearly forty-three thousand quid to earn."

He scoffed. "Rounding numbers? For shame, Eliza."

"Forty-two thousand eight hundred and fifty-eight."

"Always forgetting the pence. Do you need a piece of paper? An abacus, perhaps?"

She shoved at his shoulder. "Stop—or I'll climb in your lap right here and earn another night's payment."

Jesus. His groin tightened at the idea, cock thickening in his trousers. He shifted, hoping to ease the sudden ache, and tried to sound stern. "You'll do nothing of the sort, young lady."

He heard her breath hitch a second before she moved even closer, dash her. "Or what? Will you punish me, Lucien? I've heard about what teachers do to naughty young boys." Her fingers danced along his thigh, toward his groin. "Will you make me stand in the corner or paddle my bottom with a ruler?"

"Fuck, Eliza." He snatched her wrist before she could go higher. "Stop it."

"I can see you're hard. You want me."

"I want you, yes, but I won't act on it. Perhaps I'll visit Mollie and Ginny today instead." Even saying the words caused his cock to deflate, but Eliza needn't know that. Better she believed him a worthless degenerate than to hold out hope that he would take her virginity.

"No, I don't think you will," she said. "I think you want someone more innocent. More . . .inexperienced. A young girl who needs you to teach her what to do—"

Fire licked through his veins, and he snapped, "Cease speaking this instant."

Eliza laughed, a musical sound that felt like a caress over his

JOANNA SHUPE

bollocks, and crossed her arms. Thankfully, they rode the rest of the way in silence, Lucien holding onto his sanity by a thread.

By the time they arrived at his solicitor's place of business, he'd regained his equilibrium. He held her hand politely and helped her down to the walk. And if his touch lingered a shade too long as he assisted her inside, she didn't comment on it.

The secretary looked up as they entered. "May I help you?"

"The Duke of Blackwood and Lady Eliza Hawthorne to see Mr. Turner."

"Your Grace, my lady," the secretary said. "Good morning. Please, have a seat and I shall see if Mr. Turner is ready."

"Look," Eliza whispered when they were alone. "Is that a *ruler* on the desk? Shall we save it for later?"

God, he wanted that, but he couldn't. He *couldn't*. He was responsible for what happened to Robert, for what happened to her. She would hate him if she knew.

No matter her words, no matter how tempting the package, Lucien had to resist her. "Behave."

She chuckled and walked around the room, examining the art on the walls. "These look expensive. How much are you paying this solicitor?"

"I haven't the foggiest, actually." He had a business manager and secretary for those sorts of things.

Lucien hadn't troubled himself with the estate and businesses since Robert's death, more than happy to let others shoulder the burdens for a while. He'd failed at his responsibilities, had proven unworthy of anyone depending on him for anything, so it seemed best to step aside and let others do it.

"Your Grace," an older man said from the office doorway. "My lady. Won't you both come in?"

"Hello, Mr. Turner," Lucien said. "Thank you for seeing us."

"Of course, of course. Have a seat, if you please."

Lucien helped Eliza into a chair, then took his own. "Have you an answer for her ladyship on the late earl's estate?"

"I'm afraid there's not much good news. The will left by your ladyship's brother transferred all the assets to the next earl. No portion or entailment was set aside for you or your sister."

"Well, this was a waste of time." Slapping her hands on the armrests, Eliza started to get up out of the chair.

Lucien put his arm out to stay her. "Turner, there's nothing through her mother's family or distant relatives? Her mother's or father's will? Nothing at all?"

"No, I'm afraid not, Your Grace."

"Is there anything to be done about the current earl? Undoubtedly, Lady Eliza had possessions in the house at the time of her brother's death. Is she not entitled to get those possessions out?"

"I suppose, if we could prove they belonged to her and not the estate."

"He's likely thrown it all out," Eliza said with a frown. "Why would he keep anything five years later?"

"We won't know until we try," Lucien said. "And I'd like to have a little chat with his lordship anyway."

Turner cleared his throat to gain their attention. "Your Grace, I did learn that the current earl is having some financial difficulties. Perhaps if you offered him the right price...."

"Good work, Turner."

Lucien started to rise as Turner reached for a stack of papers on his desk. "Wait, if you please. Whilst Your Grace is here, may I return the final paperwork for the land sale?"

He dropped back into his seat. "Land sale?"

"Yes, it came through Your Grace's secretary. It's the property in Hampstead." When Lucien didn't say anything, the solicitor cleared his throat. "I...That is, I assumed you knew. It has the ducal signature on it."

Lucien held out his hand. Turner placed the papers in Lucien's grasp, then withdrew a handkerchief to blot his forehead. Looking down, Lucien quickly read the legalese, which authorized a sale of some land his grandfather had purchased up in Hampstead. If he recalled correctly, it was mainly used for sheep grazing.

He flipped to the last page and saw his signature and seal.

What in the bloody hell?

"I didn't authorize this. Is it too late to stop it?"

"Of course, Your Grace. The papers come to me to finalize and file. I can misplace that one."

"Papers?" Lucien snapped. "Plural?"

Turner pulled at his collar. "I thought you knew. That is, there have been more of them as of late, but I assumed Your Grace was offloading some assets. Paring down the estate."

Lucien couldn't speak. He was stunned. *Paring down the estate?*

"Mr. Turner," Eliza spoke up. "May we see all the papers to which you are referring? I believe His Grace would like to review any business you've conducted on his behalf for the last few years."

"Yes," Lucien said, numbly. "Quite."

CHAPTER 6

Eliza couldn't believe her eyes. "Lucien, your accounts are a mess."

After they left his solicitor, they went straight to his business manager's office. Then, after taking every book, ledger, and piece of paper associated with the Blackwood estate, he fired both his business manager and his secretary, telling them legal proceedings were to follow if he found anything amiss.

Now back at his townhouse, they were inside his study, reviewing his ledgers.

"This is unbelievable," he shouted, throwing one of the thick books against the wall. "Those miserable parasites! Selling off my land and assets to put the money in their own pockets. I'll have them strung up!"

"You most definitely should press charges," she said, reviewing the lines again. "Because they've stolen quite a bit of money from you."

"Damn it!" he yelled, tearing at his hair as if trying to rip the strands out of his head. "I should have paid better attention."

"Why didn't you?"

When he didn't immediately answer, she looked up. He was staring at the fire, his chin set at a stubborn angle. She frowned at him. "Well? Why not?"

"Because I was busy elsewhere, Eliza. I didn't want to review boring reports and add up numbers all day."

That wasn't like the Lucien she remembered. What had caused such a drastic change in him? "Busy with parties and women and such? That sort of busy?"

"You try being a reasonably attractive, wealthy duke under the age of thirty and see how easy it is to resist temptation."

His words rang false. Something else happened all those years ago. But if he wanted to lie, then she couldn't stop him. They weren't friends, and he owed her nothing more than six nights of mindless pleasure and fifty thousand pounds.

She returned to the ledger, staying quiet as he continued to brood. After a bit, he stood and went to the sideboard. "Drink?" he called.

"Yes, please. Whisky, if you have it."

A crystal tumbler containing a splash of amber liquid appeared before her eyes. "I wouldn't have taken you for a whisky girl," he said.

"No? What type of girl do I seem like?"

He dropped into the seat next to her. "I don't know. I never imagined you drinking spirits."

"I like almost everything except gin."

He shuddered. "Can't stand the stuff. Tastes like perfume."

"Exactly."

They drank in silence, while the fire crackled. It was cozy, a scene her thirteen-year-old self would've killed to experience. But so much has changed since then. She was no longer that wide-eyed girl, and this was not a romance.

She hoped Fanny was faring all right at home alone. Eliza didn't feel good about leaving her sister for too long. Nights, when Fanny slept, were different. But during the day, when Eliza returned from work, there were meals to prepare, clothes to launder. The apartment needed tidying, too. Fanny did what she could, but Dr. Humphries said her sister shouldn't tax herself, and Eliza didn't mind looking after them both.

"What are you thinking about?" he asked, shifting toward her slightly.

"My sister. She'll soon wonder where I am."

"My driver can take you home. Thank you for trying to help me untangle this mess." He gestured toward the desk and the mound of paperwork, his expression angry and dejected.

She didn't like seeing him hurt. She wanted to ease those worry lines on his brow and kiss away the frown he wore. Wanted to make him smile and laugh, hear him growl into her ear and call her angel, and feel the rough press of his fingertips in her skin.

Eliza didn't want to leave him.

She finished the rest of her drink, disgusted with herself. No matter what else, she couldn't become attached to him.

Setting the empty glass on the desk, she stood up. Then she began slipping the tiny buttons of her shirtwaist through the holes, undoing them. She'd managed five before Lucien realized what was happening.

He jerked in his seat. "Eliza, what are you playing at?"

Moving swiftly, she worked her way down her sternum, revealing more and more skin and undergarments along the way. It helped to serve as one's own lady's maid—she'd dressed and undressed herself every day for five years.

Lucien's gaze bounced around the room nervously, as if he were searching for an escape. The hand holding his drink trembled slightly. "There are servants in the house. It's not yet nighttime. What about your sister?" He swallowed hard. "This is wrong. You needn't do this. I will give you the money. Christ, Eliza. Please, I'm begging you. Fasten all those buttons at once."

Never had he said he didn't desire her.

Which meant she kept going, of course.

Her body felt feverish, her heart racing as she disrobed in front of him. With every garment that hit the floor, her blood ran hotter. Her sex grew embarrassingly damp. Was he able to tell?

His expression darkened as she popped open her corset and let it fall. The bulge behind his trousers made her mouth water, and she wondered if he would finally let her see his cock.

"This is wrong," he rasped through harsh breaths as she lifted her chemise over her head. Then he reclined in his armchair, limbs loose and sprawled, like he'd given up the fight. "But oh, fuck. Keep going. God help me, don't stop."

After untying her drawers, she removed everything below her waist in one go, leaving her bare. Lucien studied her with a hot hooded gaze, eliminating any hint of shyness she might've felt.

"Bloody hell, you're beautiful." He downed the rest of his whisky and plunked his glass down, hard. "Get on the sofa, angel."

Excitement raced through her as she went to the long sofa against the wall. Lucien stood slowly and removed his coat, then his waistcoat and cravat. Now in shirtsleeves and trousers, he approached her, a devious glint in his eye. "Spread your legs."

Her thighs parted at his command, her body ready to do whatever he said. She felt giddy and drunk, though it wasn't from whisky. It was from this gorgeous and charming man she'd adored when she was a girl.

Instead of mounting her, as she expected, he knelt on the carpet and grasped her hips. "You keep trying to seduce me. I think you need to be punished."

"Are you going to paddle me with a ruler?"

His lips twitched but he shook his head. "No, not yet. Right now I plan to lick your pussy until you cry, begging me to stop because you cannot possibly come again."

Without giving her a chance to respond, he lowered his head and ran his tongue through her slit. She sucked in a breath, while Lucien let out a long groan. "You are so wet. You truly want me, don't you, little virgin?"

"Yes," she whispered. "Please, Lucien."

Humming in his throat, he licked her again, the flat of his tongue scraping across her most sensitive area. He lapped at her, exploring, never touching the place she craved him most, that little button atop her sex that throbbed with wanting. She rocked her hips, seeking, but he held her down.

"You tortured me last night," he said, flicking the tip of his tongue around her entrance. "It's my turn to torture you. Be still."

There was no more air for talking because Lucien began using his lips and tongue on her, swirling and caressing her clitoris, and everything else disappeared. There was just his mouth and the incessant tingles racing down her spine, along her legs. Bleeding hell, this felt good.

The tension built inside her, her insides pulling taut, as he drove her higher, those warm licks and kisses like nothing she'd imagined. When he sucked her bud into his mouth, scraping it with his teeth, she exploded, the bliss overcoming her in a rush. "Oh, my God," she gasped as her walls pulsed in sheer happiness.

When it ebbed, Lucien gentled but didn't stop. Even when she grew sensitive and squirmed, he held her down and continued to lap at her. She considered protesting, but then she felt his finger probing at her entrance.

"You're soaking," he murmured. "Absolutely drenched. It's like heaven."

"Lucien," she panted. "Please."

She wasn't altogether certain what she was begging for, only that she needed more. Her body felt empty, needy, even in the aftermath of the best orgasm of her life. Was he planning to take her virginity here?

Suddenly, she wanted that more than anything else in the world.

"I'll take care of you, angel," he said, the tip of his finger sliding inside her pussy. His tongue painted her clitoris, which was swollen from earlier, and her back arched from the sensations battering her system.

"Yes, Lucien. It's so good."

The stretch of her inner tissues was strange and forbidden, a wicked touch that had her panting and rocking, trying to get him deeper. He was gentle, however, so very gentle, slowly filling her for the first time. When his finger was finally seated inside her, he rubbed a spot that made her see stars. "Blast!" she cried. "What was that?"

"Magic. Do you like it?"

He repeated the motion, and she reacted instantly, grabbing his hair and rocking her hips into his mouth, unable to help herself. It was like he'd shocked her with electric current, and her body could only react. The muscles of her stomach contracted, and he doubled his efforts, his tongue stroking quickly, and she nearly came off the sofa as another orgasm swept up and over her. Stronger than the first one, it seemed to go on and on, a never-ending cascade of ecstasy that she was powerless to stop.

When the peak ebbed, she sagged into the couch, boneless. Her throat ached from her cries. Lucien kept nibbling her folds and the crease of her thigh, his finger still embedded in her channel, and he pumped his hand lazily, mimicking what his cock would do. God, she couldn't wait.

"Please," she said, her hands scrabbling at him, trying to bring him closer.

"One more, I think." He began giving her those drugging, open-mouthed deep kisses again and her eyes rolled back in her head.

"No, Lucien. It's too much."

"You can take it, my clever girl."

He didn't let up, and she could only whine, too far gone to form words as he gave her one more orgasm. When it was over, she couldn't open her eyes, her body sore and heavy, and he finally released her. She winced as his finger withdrew, but there was a strange emptiness now, a sense that part of her was missing.

"Sleep, my darling," he said, his lips brushing her forehead.

He never found his release, was her last thought before the blackness tugged her down.

CHAPTER 7

Eliza awoke wrapped in a warm and soft cocoon, not a stitch of clothing on her body. How long had she been asleep? Dying afternoon light streamed through large bay windows she didn't recognize. An unfamiliar painted ceiling stared down, while strange furniture surrounded her.

Lucien. Ledger books. Sofa.

Ah, yes. Relaxing, she pulled the blanket tighter around her nakedness. That had been remarkable, though not quite what he'd paid for. Interesting that during his thorough ministrations, he hadn't lost control. He hadn't been overcome with need, like last night.

He hadn't come close to taking her virginity.

Was this her fate? To have the one man she'd been obsessed with for years pleasure her beyond reason, but never claim her?

He was at his desk, and she watched through her lashes as he reviewed the ducal accounting books, his hair mussed and sleeves rolled high on his forearms. He'd discarded his collar, revealing the thick column of his throat, and on his face sat a pair of thin eyeglasses. Her sex quivered. He was absolutely gorgeous, concentrating so intently that a crease had formed between his brows. She wanted to smooth it away with her thumb.

When she thought of Lucien, this was what she imagined, a serious and clever man. Dedicated and responsible, not the reprobate with two mistresses and a devil-may-care attitude. She far preferred this version.

I could love this version.

No, no, no. This was not a romance. As much as the thirteen-year-old inside her longed to fall at his feet and worship him, that was just a fantasy. Real life had taken them in different directions and she would not become his mistress. Fanny was her responsibility now.

She sat up, the blanket wrapped tight around her nakedness, and his gaze flicked toward her. Removing his eyeglasses, he said, "There you are. I was wondering how long you would sleep."

She rose and went around the desk to stand by his chair. "Your mouth should be outlawed."

The side of his mouth hitched as he leaned back in his chair. "I know."

Unable to keep from reaching out, she swept a lock of dark hair off his forehead. "Arrogant man."

He edged away and cleared his throat. "Eliza, we should talk."

"Excellent idea. Let's go up to your bedroom and talk in bed."

"Absolutely not." He pushed his chair back and stood, as if he needed to put space between them. "I have an idea."

"A naughty idea?"

"Dash it, no. Will you let me finish?" He sighed and pointed to the books on his desk. "This is a disaster. I need help sorting out the estate and you've already started working on the books with me. I'd like to hire you."

"I don't understand. You've already 'hired' me for six more nights."

"No, I haven't—and not for this. I want to offer you legitimate work. Here, for me. With the accounts."

"Oh." She looked at the desk, her mind turning this over.

"This way, we needn't do any more of *that*." He waved his hand in the direction of the sofa.

Her stomach dropped. He wasn't going to bed her. She'd thrown herself at him twice and Lucien had resisted. Now he'd found a way to pay her to *not* take her virginity.

She should've been thrilled.

She should've been grateful.

Instead, she was disappointed.

"I see."

"I . . ." He dragged a hand through his hair, mussing it even more. "I thought you'd be relieved. This way, you needn't lose your virginity. You can still marry a decent man and have a family. You needn't sleep with me for money."

But I want to sleep with you, Lucien. Badly.

It wasn't one sided, either. He admitted to wanting her. Had climaxed last night, and pounced on her when she removed her clothes earlier.

You're mine, Eliza.

Had he meant it? If so, why the sudden and annoying nobility? The man had *two* mistresses! Seducing him should not prove this damn difficult.

She considered his proposition. Working on his accounts would keep her here in the house. With him. Alone. That was a plus, unless he was determined to leave her chaste, which was a colossal minus.

Admittedly, it would be nice to put her maths skills to use. Balancing her and Fanny's meager budget each month wasn't exactly taxing her brain box. But agreeing felt like giving up on something monumental. Something she'd dreamed of for *years*.

"May I be honest with you?" she asked.

His expression wary, he folded his arms across his chest. "Of course."

"I was looking forward to more of that." She hooked a thumb at the sofa. "I was looking forward to sleeping with you."

Lips parting in surprise, he stood, frozen. "I . . .don't understand. Why? You'd be ruined."

She could only throw her head back and laugh. "Lucien, I don't care about my maidenhead or my reputation. Those things matter in Mayfair, not in the real world. And in case you haven't noticed, I like doing these things with you. I . . . " God, was she really going to confess this? "I had a crush on you as a girl. This is actually fulfilling some of my fantasies."

He dragged both hands through his hair, appearing aggravated at her revelation. "Do not tell me these things. Your brother would cut off my bollocks with a rusty knife, Eliza."

"He's not here, but I am. I'll help you with your accounts, but I want to do the rest, too."

"Why are you insisting on this? I thought you would be grateful."

"Do you desire me, Lucien?"

"I shouldn't answer that."

Which was an answer unto itself. Still, she had to push. One thing Eliza had learned in the last five years was to take charge of her life, not to let an obstacle in her path deter her.

And right now, that obstacle was Lucien's nobility.

She dropped the blanket. "Do you want to fuck me, Lucien?"

The air in the room turned heavy and thick, making it impossible to breathe. He hardly moved, and the hunger in his expression sent a torrent of heat along her veins, causing her core to pulse with desire.

"You know I do," he growled.

"Then prove it."

* * *

ROBERT WOULD PUNCH Lucien in the face were he still alive.

Lucien tried to resist, but he inhaled and caught the scent of Eliza's arousal, and he was lost, drowning in a sea of longing. He hadn't washed his face from earlier, either, and the taste of her lingered on his tongue, on his skin. Christ, he wanted her.

She stood there patiently, as bare as the day she was born, waiting for him to make up his mind. The curve of her hip beckoned, the perfect place to hold onto whilst he explored her body. Then he studied the slope of her breast, the swell of her belly. His cock throbbed in his trousers, insistent and annoying, and the temptation was more than he could bear.

This was terrible. *He* was terrible—spoiled and selfish, used to getting what he wanted—and his body hated to be denied. After all, he'd paid for her innocence. The idea of feeling her virgin cunt strangle his cock...

He closed his eyes briefly. Why wouldn't she take the fifty thousand pounds, buy a house in Mayfair, and everything could return to the way it was before? The last five years would disappear. Why did she insist on torturing him like this?

Why must she insist on giving him her virginity?

His body didn't care about the reasons at present. She was naked and asking him to fuck her, and he didn't think he was capable of refusing her a damn thing. His fingers curled into fists.

I shouldn't.

She deserves better.

She will hate me when she learns what happened to her brother.

The devil in him, however, began rationalizing.

One night. Afterwards, she would help him with his accounts. He would give her the money and ease his conscience. She would restart her life like nothing ever happened.

"You'll help me with the accounts? After we sleep together once?"

"Yes."

"And you'll accept the money?"

"In exchange for my virginity and five days of accounting, yes."

"Five days! This will take longer than that."

"I agreed to only seven nights, Lucien. You'll get no more." She stretched her arms toward the ceiling, her perfect apple-shaped breasts rising. Her nipples were hard little points begging for his mouth.

Distracted, he lost his train of thought. "Wait, why?"

"Because I have a life and responsibilities outside of you. Shocking, I know."

"But...."

"But, nothing. You already have two mistresses. You don't require a third."

He hadn't seen those two mistresses in days, had lost interest in them because of Eliza, who at the moment was moving toward him, her hips swaying and breasts bouncing. The urge to bite all that perfect skin, to mark her as his own, had his hands shaking.

When she reached him, she trailed her finger down his throat, between his collarbones. "You claim my virginity tonight, then we move on to business tomorrow. Everyone wins."

"No taking it back once it's done," he warned.

"I won't regret it. Deep down, I always wanted it to be you."

Jesus Christ.

Hesitation evaporated like morning dew in the hot sun. Spinning, he found his topcoat on the chair. In a flash, he wrapped her in it, then lifted her in his arms. She clutched at his shoulders, laughing. "Where are we going?"

"Upstairs."

Then they were in the corridor, his leather shoes slapping the marble floor on their way to the staircase. The footman in the front hall quickly averted his eyes, expression unchanging, as if his employer held a naked woman in his arms every day. Despite his reputation, though, this was a first. Lucien never fucked women here.

Just Eliza, apparently.

She'd grown bolder these last few years, nothing like the young girl who used to blush when he stared at her a few seconds too long from across a dining table. Yet she was still so innocent.

A combination that hardened his cock beyond reason.

Once in his bedroom, he strode to the bed and tossed her on top. She bounced, chuckling, and he began tearing off his clothing, desperate to feel her bare skin against his own. Coming to her knees, she shuffled forward to help, her eager fingers starting with his trousers.

They worked together until he was naked, then he let her look her fill. His erection stood out proudly, eagerly, and he half-expected her to change her mind. "Are you sure, Eliza?"

She looked at his cock and reached a tentative hand toward it, all wide-eyed curiosity and fascination. "Very."

Oh, God. If she touched him, he wouldn't last.

He pointed to the bed. "On your back. Spread your legs."

She hurried to comply, limbs scrambling in her haste. Now it was his turn to look his fill, never wishing to forget the way she appeared in his bed. No lover had ever visited his home before, and he anticipated smelling her on his sheets afterward.

One night. That was all.

He crawled onto the mattress, up between her thighs, which he shoved wider to make room for himself. Her pussy gleamed in the firelight, her slickness like a sweet treat just waiting to be devoured. "I'm going to prepare you, so relax. Understand?"

"Yes," she said on an exhale of breath.

Without waiting another second, he lowered his head and nuzzled her. This couldn't be rushed. He teased the edges of her sex with his nose and lips. When she shifted impatiently, he gave a gentle lick through her seam, stopping just below her clitoris.

Then he applied himself to the task, using his tongue in creative ways—back and forth, circling, pressing—until she was panting. Her fingers found their way into his hair and she held on, her hips rocking, churning, seeking . . .and it took everything he had not to surge up and ram his cock inside her. He had to go gently.

A mewling sound escaped her throat, while her nails dug into his scalp. "Now, Lucien. Please."

The need in his body doubled, tripled, and he had to close his eyes before he began humping the bed in desperation. He sucked her clitoris between his lips and flicked it with his tongue. Gasping, she tensed and let out a moan, the sweetest sound he'd ever heard.

"It's not enough, Lucien. I need you."

Moving a finger toward her channel, he pushed gently inside, the walls sucking him in greedily. Fuck, she was tight. Hot. Slick. He growled into her flesh, every muscle clenched in agony as he tried to stem the hunger clawing inside him. Sweet Eliza, with her spine of steel and mind for numbers. He could get used to her taste, the way she swelled on his tongue. How she gripped his hair in her fist to keep his mouth where she wanted.

He could do this for the rest of his life and die a happy man.

"More, Lucien. Please."

He rose up over her as he slid another finger inside her. "Yes, my lovely girl. You're so very tight, but I'm going to fill you up."

Remembering her reaction on the sofa, he crooked his fingers inside her, and she jolted, letting out a loud moan. "There we go, angel," he crooned. "That's my favorite spot."

Soon, he wedged a third finger in her channel. This was a tighter squeeze, so he distracted her with a deep kiss, until he had the digits seated inside her. Damn, she was snug. He imagined all that heat strangling his shaft and nearly came right then.

"Oh, God. Please, now. Lucien, I'm ready." Her hands pulled at him. "Please."

He reached for the drawer next to the bed and found the package containing a shield. It took only a second or two to roll the thick rubber onto his shaft. Then he took a vial out of the drawer.

"What is that?" she panted.

"Oil. It will help me slide inside you."

He poured a small amount into his hands, set the vial down, then smeared the oil on his rubber-covered shaft, trembling at the sensation. He wasn't certain how long he could last.

Clenching his jaw to keep from spending, he lined up at her entrance and pushed forward, making certain to watch the slow invasion. His hands held her hips steady as her entrance gave way and sucked the crown inside. "That's it, darling. Take me in. Be my very good girl and take my cock inside you."

When she tensed, his gaze darted to hers. "Easy," he said, stroking her thigh. "I'm going to take care of you."

Using his thumb, he drew circles over her clitoris and her muscles eased, relaxed, which allowed Lucien to sink deeper into her sex. They both groaned. This gentle advance went on for several minutes as he invaded and conquered, stroked and petted. Wet heat surrounded him, strangled his shaft, and his brain struggled to keep up.

"More, please," she whispered and tilted her hips higher. "I need you deep inside me, where I ache."

Gritting his teeth against the need to ram inside her, he said, "I don't want to hurt you."

She wrapped her arms around his waist, then slid them lower, grabbing his buttocks. Then she sunk her nails into his backside, hard.

He hissed at the exquisite pain and his hips snapped, driving her into the mattress, their bodies fully joined. She squeaked, almost recoiling, and guilt slammed through him. "Goddamn it, Eliza. I'm sorry." He held perfectly still, his lids squeezed tightly against the absolute bliss of being fully sheathed. "I didn't mean to enter you so quickly. Are you all right?"

"I'm fine. Stop worrying." She wriggled slightly beneath him. "It was a pinch but now it's done."

"I should pull out." He started to shove up off the mattress, but she clutched him harder, digging those nails into his skin once more. He shivered.

"Don't you dare. Teach me, Lucien. Tell me what you like, what makes you come."

Groaning, he shoved his face into the soft skin of her throat. "No, no, no. Stop talking." His hips began rocking, pleasure coursing down his spine. "Fuck, Eliza. I need to make this last. I need to make this good for you."

"This isn't about me," she whispered, the vixen. "You bought me, paid for my virginity. I'm yours to do with whatever you please."

Goddamn it. Lust shot through his groin and along his cock. This was wrong. All of this was so bloody wrong.

He began thrusting then, sweat gathering on his skin, and the bed rocked with the force of his movements. "It's so good . . .you feel so good. Tight. Oh, God, so bloody tight."

"*Yes*," she moaned near his ear. "Keep going. I'm yours, Lucien. Only yours."

Whatever restraint he'd been clinging to deserted him. Pushing up, he grabbed her hands and pinned them to the mattress, holding her down as he continued to pound into her. He felt like an animal, a beast mindlessly rutting. "Do you like it? Do you like the way a cock feels inside you?"

Her walls clenched around his length, giving him her answer. "Yes, yes, yes," she chanted, her face awash in pleasure, making him feel like the most powerful man on earth. "Just yours, Lucien."

Satisfaction filled him. He was the first man to fuck this glorious creature, the first to see her expression twist in euphoria as he thrust inside her. He made certain to brush her clitoris with his pelvic bone on every stroke. His hands kept her where he wanted, but she didn't try to pull free, as if she liked being at his mercy.

A million pricks of fire exploded in his veins. "You're mine now," he said, his voice thick. "Mine to fuck whenever I want. Perhaps I'll tie you to my bed, naked, spread open so you'll always be ready for me. Ready to take my cock."

She must've liked that because her core spasmed around his length, as if she were trying to pull him deeper inside. Her shout filled the room as she came.

"Goddamn it." He couldn't hold out any longer. His hips stuttered, grew uncoordinated, and he threw his head back to roar at the ceiling. Jets of spend filled the rubber and every muscle twitched in blissful agony. When his thoughts realigned moments later, he stared down at her gorgeous face and saw her satisfied expression. His stomach instantly sank.

Oh, shit. What had he done?

CHAPTER 8

*E*liza floated for a bit after, contentment rippling throughout her limbs as they lay there, still joined. Lucien panted, his face relaxed, making him appear younger, more like the man she once knew. The man she'd once dreamt about marrying. Her heart quivered, then turned over in her chest. She had the sudden urge to wrap around him and never let go.

Sharing his bed had been so much more than she imagined, like he'd taken her apart and rearranged her, an equation that no longer made sense. One only he could solve. And, she craved more of him and their intimacies.

Damnation. This was a fiasco.

She pushed his shoulder and he obliged, falling to his back on the mattress with a thud. The shield still covered his softening erection, and his spend was making a mess of him and the bedclothes. Apt, considering how the afternoon had gone. She'd made a mess of everything.

Worse, she'd agreed to return tomorrow.

She had to resist the temptation, because this affection, this blooming emotion towards him would only grow worse. What happened at the end of the seven days? Would she fall in love with him? Agree to be his mistress, anything for another crumb of his attention?

She absolutely couldn't risk it. Yes, he'd taken her virginity, which was the fulfillment of so many of her girlhood dreams. Now she would straighten out the ducal accounts and help him set things to rights. Then, she would disappear from his life with her heart intact.

"I should go," she blurted and shoved up off the bed.

"Wait." He reached for her. "Let me take care of you. Clean you up and make sure you're not hurt."

Dread clogged her throat. Any hint of tenderness would do her in right now. The walls between this man and her heart had taken a beating moments ago, nearly crumbling, and she needed time and space to rebuild and reinforce them.

"I'm right as rain, duke." She removed her arm from his grasp and lunged for his silk dressing gown on the chair. "You needn't fuss over me."

"Eliza, goddamn it." He sat up and dealt with the shield. "Don't rush out of here again. I want to talk about this."

Lord, that was almost a worse idea than the bloody tenderness.

Besides, she had to get home to her sister.

Throwing her arms into the oversized sleeves, she started babbling on her way to the door. "Lovely time, must run. You were amazing. The stuff of poetry, really. Talk more later. Sweet dreams. Good night."

"Do not dare—"

She closed the door behind her and hurried toward the stairs. Humiliating that her clothing was in his study, but there was no help for it now. She had to quickly dress and find a hack. Fanny would be worried sick if Eliza wasn't home before dark.

Lucien had collected her things into a pile, bless him, so she began dragging the pieces on. Just as she fastened her corset, the door opened and the duke stormed in, his face a picture of unhappiness. He wore trousers, a shirt and waistcoat, and carried a pair of shoes and a topcoat in his hands. "So you were planning on sneaking out again? Is that it?"

"I said goodbye. I was hardly sneaking."

"I know someone desperate for escape when I see it, Eliza." He dragged on his coat. "Shall I tie you to my bed, or are you going to answer me honestly right here?"

Her mouth went dry and she had to drag in a deep breath, the words appealing to her in ways she would never have guessed two hours ago. "I must return home to my sister." It was true, after all.

He studied her face as if searching for a lie. "I called for my carriage already, so I will take you."

"No, I'd rather—"

"You'd rather take a hack or a tram. I know, but I won't allow it. So short of poisoning or stabbing me, that won't happen."

"You should return to your books. They need your help far worse than I do."

"The books may wait. I will ensure you get home safely first."

And I must put distance between us before I fall in love with you.

She tried to reason with him as she fastened her skirts. "I'll allow your driver to see me home if you stay here."

"Absolutely not. I'm not letting you go all the way to Shoreditch alone. End of discussion."

"You're being absurd."

"And you're being stubborn." Once he shoved his feet into his shoes, he folded his arms, blocking her only path to escape with his body. "I'll gladly carry you to the carriage. Your choice."

She glared at him as she buttoned her shirtwaist. "Are you like this with all your lovers, or merely me?"

"Just you, it appears. Ready?"

There was no getting out of it that she could see, so she followed him to the large fancy carriage and piled in. He sat across from her, their knees touching, and heat curled in her belly. Every bounce of the springs reminded her that Lucien had just taken her virginity.

She must've winced, because he asked, "Are you sore?"

Her chest expanded, like her heart was swelling. The urge to crawl into his lap and let him hold her roared inside her. "I'm fine. Just a bit tired. Mind if I sleep?"

His gaze narrowed as if he didn't believe her. "You wouldn't be trying to ignore me, would you?"

"No," she lied. "I'm exhausted. You've worn me out."

"Then sleep. I'll wake you once we're there."

She thought to close her eyes for a few moments, but she must've truly fallen asleep because Lucien was suddenly shaking her awake. The carriage had stopped.

"We've arrived," his deep voice said, the expression in his eyes so soft and adoring that she nearly kissed him.

Pushing up, she straightened. He'd ordered the carriage directly to her lodgings, which meant . . . "You discovered where I live. How?"

"I've been waiting for you to ask me that all day. I had a man waiting outside my home last night, just in case someone visited me to collect on one of her evenings."

Dash it. She'd led Lucien right to her. "Bully for you, then." She reached over him to push the latch on the carriage door. "I'll see you in the morning."

He stepped down and held out his hand. Confusion furrowed her brows. "What are you doing?"

"Escorting you inside."

She barely stifled her gasp. She couldn't imagine his reaction to her humble apartment. It would mortify her beyond belief. "Absolutely not."

"If you want to make it inside, it will be with me at your side. Come, Eliza."

"You needn't worry over my virtue. You've taken care of that already, duke."

"This has nothing to do with your virtue or reputation. This is about your safety. Now, must I carry you?"

"Stop threatening to carry me," she snapped. "It's tiresome."

In a flash, he grabbed her forearms, yanked her forward, and hauled her over his shoulder. "I'll return shortly," he called to his driver.

She was draped over him like a carpet, her legs dangling while he cradled the backs of her thighs. "You obnoxious toff. Put me down this bloody instant."

He had the nerve to smack her bottom. "Quiet, impudent baggage."

"That's the way, guv!" a female voice shouted out from a window above them.

"You're welcome to slap my bottom anytime, sir," another woman called.

Thankfully, they were soon inside her building. "Which floor?" he asked, his voice clipped.

"Four—and there's no elevator, so have a jolly time carrying me up all those steps."

"I've carried pillows that are heavier than you."

Lucien proved his excellent physical condition by taking the four flights easily, not even sounding winded. "Which one?"

"Second on the right."

After he stomped over, jostling her, he knocked on the door.

"This is humiliating," she muttered.

"I told you I wanted to take care of you," he said. "I saw your wince in the carriage."

Her skin heated, partly embarrassment but mostly pleasure. This caring and possessive side of him was nearly irresistible.

The door opened.

"Is that . . . ." Fanny sounded confused. "Is that my sister over your shoulder?"

"Lady Fanny," Lucien said. "If you'll allow me in, I'll drop off this parcel and be on my way."

Parcel? Eliza huffed. So much for the caring and possessive Lucien. "Put me down, you oaf."

"Your Grace," Fanny said, a hint of disapproval in her voice. "Come in."

"Thank you." He strode in, bent down, and put Eliza on her feet.

"Was that necessary?" she asked him.

"I think so, yes."

Fanny's worried gaze looked the duke over first, then Eliza, and Eliza could see the wheels turning in her sister's head, putting the pieces in place. Of course, with Lucien half-dressed, higher level reasoning wasn't exactly required.

"Is Your Grace planning to stay for dinner?" Fanny asked. "We have soup."

Eliza didn't give him a chance to answer. "No, he's leaving. Good night, Lucien. I will see you in the morning."

"Ladies," he said with a perfectly executed bow. "I'll leave you to your evening."

Then he departed and the silence in the apartment was deafening. The sisters stared at one another for so long, they heard Lucien's carriage pull away.

"You have feelings for him," Fanny finally said.

"That's absurd." Though Eliza suspected it wasn't.

"We should rethink this plan, because I will never forgive myself if my illness forces you to become some toff's mistress."

"I'm not going to become his mistress. It's only five days and I'm only helping him with some accounting matters. No intimacy required. Furthermore, we agreed on this. It's the best way to get the money and then sail to America."

Before that happened, Eliza had to earn her fifty thousand pounds.

Fanny narrowed her eyes and opened her mouth—to continue arguing, no doubt—but she coughed instead. Deep wracking coughs that crackled in her chest. Even though it was warm in the apartment, Eliza closed the window, trying to keep the dirty London air out for the moment. Fanny needed clean air, which was scarce in the city.

When Fanny caught her breath, she continued their conversation as if the coughing fit never happened. "Just promise me you won't fall in love with him."

"I promise."

For the rest of the night, Eliza feared she'd already broken that promise.

* * *

THE DUCAL BOOKS were even worse off than Eliza first believed. That Lucien allowed things to get this bad was absolutely appalling.

And quite unlike the man she remembered from all those years ago.

What happened to him?

She hadn't seen the duke in three and a half days. Instead, she came to his home, sat in his office, and poured through the accounting ledgers. The books hadn't been updated in some time, and there were strange entries she didn't understand. Those she noted on a separate piece of paper to ask him about.

She tried not to think about him, but it was hard when she was surrounded by reminders of him all day long.

You're mine now. Mine to fuck whenever I want.

Heat suffused her, as it did every time she considered Lucien's words. She dared not tell Fanny any of the details. Hearing how gloriously rough and filthy Lucien was in bed wouldn't reassure Fanny that Eliza would keep her vow never to become his mistress.

And honestly, Eliza wasn't certain she wanted to tell anyone. Not right now, at least. There were lonely years ahead of her in which she could try to make sense of him and the last few days.

In the meantime, she'd enjoy the work, the challenge to her brain, while sitting in a fine Mayfair home again, where it was warm and smelled nice. She wasn't on her knees scrubbing, or leaning over to sew in candlelight. Perhaps Lucien could write her a letter of recommendation, too, one that would allow her to find employment in an American accounting firm.

Where was he anyway? Was he intending not to see her at all before the end of the five days?

The possibility sent a pang through her chest. She hadn't expected that. When she agreed to help him with the books, she assumed they would be side-by-side, laughing and talking as they worked. Not with her cooped up alone while he did whatever it was he did all day.

Was he with his mistresses?

The pang sounded again, the pressure on her sternum like a

JOANNA SHUPE

boulder had been dropped there. She tried to remind herself that she held no claim over him. *I cannot be jealous. He is not mine.*

Besides, tomorrow was her last day here.

Afterwards, they'd both return to their lives, and Eliza would focus on Fanny's recovery. They would find an American sanitarium to accept Fanny and heal her. Then they would buy a house and settle somewhere with plenty of fresh air and sunshine.

So it shouldn't bother her if Lucien wished to ignore her. The more time they spent together would make it harder to separate tomorrow.

And yet, she couldn't stop glancing at the door every few minutes, waiting for it to pop open and reveal his handsome face.

Then the door did open. Eliza straightened, a hopeful smile twisting her lips . . .which dimmed when a footman appeared with a tray. She swallowed her disappointment.

"Your lunch, my lady."

"Michael, as I told you yesterday and the day before, you may call me Eliza. Or Miss Hartsford."

He shook his head. "His Grace's orders. We address you properly, as befitting your station."

Oh, that dratted annoying man.

"Can you tell me, is His Grace here today?"

"Yes, miss."

"I see."

He was here, yet he hadn't stopped in to say hello. Were they no longer friends now that he'd taken her virginity? Was her hymen all he'd wanted, like some sort of trophy or prize? Hurt and anger swirled in her belly, twisting and turning, until the urge to yell at him rose to a fever pitch. "Where is he?"

The skin above the footman's collar turned a deep red. "I probably shouldn't say, my lady. His Grace asked to be left alone."

"I understand. I wouldn't like for you to lose your position." Finding work was a miserable endeavor, and as much as she wished to see Lucien, she wouldn't do it at an employee's expense. "Thank you for the tray."

"Your ladyship is most welcome."

When the footman left, Eliza waited a few minutes, then set off exploring. It shouldn't be terribly hard to find Lucien. The townhouse was large, but it wasn't a labyrinth. She would conduct a systematic search of every floor, avoiding the areas reserved for the staff.

She decided to start on the ground floor, then work her way up. Moving quickly and quietly, she explored but found only empty rooms. On the first floor, his bedroom was quiet and still. Same for the other bedrooms. As she passed the ballroom, however, a thumping sound caught her notice.

Carefully, she cracked the door and peered inside. Her lips parted on a surprised exhale. A bare-chested Lucien was pummeling a large canvas bag, his hands wrapped in cloth. Sweat rolled down his skin, his muscles popping with his rapid movements.

Sweet heavens. She couldn't tear her gaze away. He was stunning, a Greek god come to life to make mortal men appear like flabby, inconsequential fools. Arousal tightened her nipples into points, the area between her legs tingling as she watched. The minutes dragged on and she began to worry she'd melt into a puddle on the floor. All that would be left was some threadbare clothing and hair pins.

She desired him. Right now.

It wasn't easy to admit, but Eliza knew when she'd been beaten. Her resistance crumbled like grains of sand. What was one more time when her heart already belonged to him?

She closed the door behind her, which caused him to pause midpunch and glance over. His chest heaved as he panted. "What are you doing here?"

"Coming to find you."

"Why?" He wiped his forehead with the back of his hand. "Is there a problem downstairs?"

There was a problem all right, and it had to do with the ache inside her that only he could satisfy.

"Are you avoiding me?" As she approached, he went over to pick up a cloth from the floor. "Because I haven't seen you in three and a half days."

"I'm busy, Eliza." He wiped his face with the cloth. "You've been making excellent progress, though."

"You've been looking at the books after I leave, then."

"Yes."

"Why not look at them with me? Then we may discuss any questions I have."

His hands rested on his hips, making his bare chest appear impossibly wide. "Just leave the questions and I'll get to them when I can."

Why was he being so cagey?

Ignoring his deep frown, she closed the distance between them. The heat from his body was like a furnace, and she longed to touch all that sweat and strength. "I was thinking . . ." She licked her lips as a bead of sweat trickled down the center of his chest. "Tomorrow is our last day together."

"And?"

"And it would be a shame to waste it, hiding in the ballroom."

"I'm not hiding," he said, his voice sounding strangled as she caught a bead of his sweat on her fingertip before it could reach his stomach. "And you shouldn't be in here."

"Am I still yours, Lucien?"

The whispered question echoed in the empty room, and a muscle worked in his jaw as they stared at one another. *Say yes,* she thought. *Please say yes.*

"Eliza—"

"It's a simple question. Am I still yours?"

"It doesn't matter. I cannot keep you. It's best if we maintain our distance until you finish tomorrow."

"It does matter. It matters at this moment."

"Why? Because you're trying to torture me?"

She placed her palm on his jaw and stroked the heavy whiskers he hadn't shaved off today. "Because I want you to take me to your bed one more time."

CHAPTER 9

Surprisingly, Lucien didn't put up a fight. He merely grabbed her hand and tugged her through his house as if they'd done this a hundred times. She didn't bother hiding in embarrassment. What was the point? He'd taken her virginity already and her body was burning alive, desperate for him. Let the servants talk. She'd never see them again after tomorrow anyway.

You're mine now.

How she wished it were true. To wake up with him every day, roll over into his arms and find his warm hard body. To laugh with him and discuss maths at the dinner table. To have days and months and years together, their memories and hearts intertwined.

But those were just fantasies.

Lucien wasn't for her. Dukes married girls from the very best families, not girls who once scrubbed privies and mopped vomit off the floor. Certainly not a girl who sold her virginity in a club full of aristocratic gentlemen.

Do not fall in love with him, Fanny had warned.

Too late. It felt like Eliza had loved Lucien for so long that it was hard to remember a time when she hadn't. Sharing his bed had caused those feelings to multiply exponentially. Leaving him was going to kill her.

When his bedchamber door closed, she threw herself at him, wasting no time in sealing her mouth to his. He met her kiss eagerly, and her hands skated over his bare torso. He felt divine, big and hot.

"I have to fuck you." He began walking her toward the wall while gathering her skirts in his hand. "It will be fast and hard, so please tell me you aren't too sore."

"Not sore. Please, Lucien. Hurry."

He growled and lunged for her mouth again, his tongue thrusting inside to flick and rub against hers as cool air hit her stocking-covered legs. "Put your legs around my waist," he said and lifted under her buttocks until her thighs were splayed, her knees hugging his hips.

"That's it," he crooned and, after some maneuvering with his clothing, the head of his cock nudged her entrance. "Let me in, my darling girl. I'm going to take such good care of you."

Oh, heavens. The temptation of those words. She couldn't let herself believe them.

This was all, right here. Today and tomorrow. Then they'd go their separate ways—Lucien back to his two mistresses and Eliza to America.

Even if she couldn't keep him, she'd ensure he remembered her long after she'd gone.

"I like when you take care of me," she whispered. "I like when you teach me, too. Will you spank me and put me in the corner if I'm a naughty student?"

"Goddamn it," he gritted out from between clenched teeth and shoved halfway inside her, as if he couldn't help himself. "You drive me out of my bloody mind."

It was not an easy fit, and she was impatient to lose herself in him. "More," she begged. "I need all of you."

With a grunt, he flexed his hips and drove up until he was fully seated. She gasped, her nails digging into his shoulders, as her body adjusted. "Good lord, Lucien."

"Shh, you can take me." He held still, his big body pinning her to the wall, hands under her thighs. "You were made for my cock, Eliza."

She doubted it. At the moment, it felt as if he would snap her in two. Still, she loved the feeling of having Lucien inside her, his thick shaft filling her and stealing her breath. A small bite of pain chased by immense pleasure.

So much pleasure.

"Please," she whispered into his throat. "Please, you have to move. I am dying to feel you."

"Is that so?" His voice was low and tight, like she wasn't the only one suffering. "Is your pussy greedy for me?"

Her lids fell as her head dropped onto his shoulder. Did all dukes speak in such a filthy manner, or just hers?

"Yes," she answered, wriggling her hips. "So greedy. I need you."

He gave a small thrust, and tiny sparkles raced along her spine. Her walls gripped him, unwilling to let him go, but he withdrew and pushed forward, rocking back and forth, until they built a steady rhythm. His mouth hovered over hers, his hot breath warming her skin, and she could feel him everywhere, inside and out, drowning her, and she never wanted to breathe air again. "Oh, God," she said on a moan as he ground into her, bliss echoing in every cell, every muscle.

"Would you like to learn something new?"

"Yes, please."

He carried her to the bed. "Roll over, then get up on your hands and knees."

Keeping her skirts above her waist, she did as he asked. "Like this?" She glanced over her shoulder.

With his stare locked on the slit of her drawers, he tucked his hard cock into his trousers, but didn't touch her. Instead, he went to the small secretary against the wall and opened a drawer. When she saw what he took out, her whole body quivered.

A ruler.

"You've been very bad." As he approached the bed, he smacked the hard wooden stick against his palm. "Teasing me and making me want to fuck you."

Sweet Jesus, was he truly going to spank her? She'd mentioned this in jest, but now she wasn't so sure. "What are you doing?"

His smile was sinister as he stepped just off to the side. "Giving you your punishment. Aren't you curious to know what it will feel like to have this hard ruler strike your bottom, my naughty girl?"

She hesitated. Yes, she was a bit curious, but she also wasn't keen on pain. "Will it hurt?"

"For only a second." He dragged his palm over one of her buttocks, then drew his fingers along her seam, making her squirm. "But the burn will turn into something bright and pleasurable, like your skin is shimmering. Glowing. Will you let me teach you? I think you're going to like it."

She likely would have agreed to anything in that moment, as long as he kept using that deep seductive voice. "All right."

Before she could even brace for it, he struck her backside with the wooden ruler. Fire roared across her skin. That smarted, her thin undergarment doing seemingly nothing to protect her.

He put a hand on her back, holding her still. "Good girl, there's one. Only nine more to go."

"Nine!" She tried to turn toward him, but his grip didn't budge, and another strike landed in a different spot. She inhaled sharply.

"That's it," he said. "Let the pain warm your skin. Then I'm going to fuck you and it will feel so very good."

The place where he'd first spanked her didn't hurt any longer. Instead, it pulsed, the entire area hot. She quite liked it.

"Can you take more?" When she nodded, he gave her two brisk slaps. It was over quickly, and she moaned at the resulting buzz in her veins as moisture collected between her thighs.

"Dirty girl, you cannot help yourself, can you? Taking off your clothes and begging me to give you my cock. You're so very needy, aren't you?"

After another smack, she was panting, shifting, her arousal at a fever pitch. "I do need you, Lucien. Please."

"Mmm, I can see your pussy dripping from here. You are an eager little thing, aren't you?" Another slap of the ruler, this time across the back of her thigh. She waited out the sharp pricks of misery until they eased and bloomed into something wonderful. Instead of holding her, he was petting her spine. "If you beg me properly, I might fuck you again."

"Oh, please. Please fuck me, Your Grace."

Two spanks right together. "And you're not going to tease me any longer?"

"No, Your Grace."

He gave her another hard smack. "That is for calling me Your Grace."

Before she could say anything else, he roughly pulled her hips closer with one hand. Then the head of his cock met her entrance and he was back inside her. "Jesus fuck, you're wet."

His palms slid inside the slit of her drawers to cup the red-hot abused skin. He squeezed, causing a fresh wave of pain to roll through her, but it quickly turned to a blissful throb. Finally he started moving, driving, pounding, rattling her bones with his powerful thrusts.

Whimpering, she clawed at the bedclothes. This angle brought him deeper, rubbing a certain spot with every drive of his hips, and the sound of their slapping bodies filled the room. Her skin vibrated, a reminder of what he'd done with the ruler, and it quickly became too much. "Oh, God. Don't stop . . ." The orgasm streaked through her, fierce and bright, a flash of sparks against a night sky, and she shouted, her walls clenching around his length as she trembled.

"You're so beautiful," he gasped, holding perfectly still and panting against her back. "You've always been so goddamn beautiful." He snapped his hips once. "I love the way you make me feel. Never leave me, my clever girl."

Her toes curled in blissful happiness. It was the most he'd ever revealed of his feelings for her, and the words sank in to fill the holes in her lonely heart. If only she could stay with him. "I'm yours, Lucien."

He began riding her fast and rough then, his cock punching into her sex until he pressed tight, his fingertips digging into her hips. "Fuck, Eliza!" he shouted to the ceiling. "You're *mine*." Suddenly, he swelled inside her, his body straining as he grunted with pleasure.

When it was over, she collapsed on the bed. Lucien's forehead rested on her back, his warm pants heating her spine through her clothing. "I forgot a shield," he said.

Oh.

The image filled her mind—a small boy or girl with his eyes and a keen ability for maths—and her heart twisted. If only. Some other lucky woman would marry him and bear his children. Watch him roll around on the floor to play with his son or daughter and hear their laughter.

She moved, sliding out from underneath him. "We should've been more careful."

"I'm sorry." He dragged a hand through his hair and dropped onto the mattress, disheveled and beautiful. "I don't have any diseases, if you're concerned. But Eliza, if there are consequences . . ."

She waited for him to finish. When he didn't, she knew why. There was no future between them, not in the ways that mattered.

Though it was for the best, that *hurt*.

I've survived worse. I'll survive this, too.

She willed her insides to freeze, forced her heart to toughen up. "You needn't worry about consequences," she promised, suddenly grateful for Helen's advice the night of the auction. Having a duke's bastard would add another burden onto her and Fanny's future they could scant afford, even with fifty thousand pounds in their pockets.

"You can't know that." He grimaced. "Even with a shield, it's possible. And your brother would not have wanted that for you."

It was telling that his only concern was in disappointing her long-dead brother. Why was Lucien so focused on the past when the present was what mattered?

She decided to tell him the truth. Perhaps then he would see her as an adult woman, not Robert's little sister. "There are places where a woman can procure a tonic to prevent conception. I plan to buy one after tomorrow."

A flash of surprise crossed his face before he masked it. "I see."

"I should return downstairs."

Just as she took a step toward the door, he grabbed her hand. "Why not stay and let me fuck you again?" He pressed a kiss to the inside of her wrist. "I'll remove your clothing and do it properly this time."

She shouldn't.

There were the ledgers and Fanny and the miles between Shoreditch and Mayfair . . .but bloody hell, Eliza wanted more of him. Enough to last the rest of her life.

Once more could not make things worse. She already loved him. After tomorrow, she'd never see him again, so better to gather all these memories while she could.

Stepping back, she began unfastening her bodice, giving her best attempt at a sultry smile. "Whatever Your Grace wishes."

* * *

EARLY THE NEXT MORNING, Lucien lifted the brass knocker and rapped it several times. It took longer than expected, but the door finally opened to reveal a maid. "Yes?"

"The Duke of Blackwood to see his lordship."

"His lordship is not receiving callers at the moment."

"He will see me." Lucien presented a card. "Tell him to come down or I will pull him out of bed myself."

The maid begrudgingly opened the door. "Wait in there," she said, gesturing to a front room.

Lucien entered, removed his gloves, and glanced about. Robert's former home was a pitiful sight. The once vibrant townhouse was dour, with bare walls and dirty floors. Lucien remembered flowers and laughter, family portraits and the smell of lemons. Those things were gone now.

The current earl, Lucien had learned, was a gambler and an idiot. He'd used the title to borrow funds on credit, and hadn't yet been able to pay any of it back. There were rumors of more loans through unscrupulous means, which meant serious consequences—the deadly kind—if they weren't paid back.

After what the new earl had done to Eliza and Fanny, Lucien couldn't bring himself to care. His only interest was in discovering if anything was still here for the two sisters.

Heavy feet on the front stairs caught his attention. Seconds later a bleary-eyed man entered, his necktie an absolute disgrace. "Blackwood," he said, as if they'd been introduced before. Which they hadn't. "What's this about?"

Lucien put a fair deal of menace in his voice as he said, "Justice."

"I beg your pardon?"

"By a twist of fate, you inherited this house, this title—neither of which you deserved—but you made a grave error when you turned your cousins out into the streets."

Barnett's lip curled. "You mean those two girls? They weren't my problem. Let one of the other relatives take care of them."

"Only a bloody monster would cast two young women into the streets of London without seeing them provided for, while telling everyone they went to an aunt in Scotland."

Possibly sensing Lucien's rage, Barnett edged around the back of the sofa, out of arm's reach. "Those two weren't my concern. For all I knew there was an aunt in Scotland. Besides, all they had to do was marry or find some rich man to keep them as a mistress—"

Lucien lunged. In one swift motion, he snatched Barnett's throat in his fist and pinned the earl against the wall. "You miserable piece of filth. They were mere girls—and your cousins. I am going to ruin you." He shook the other man. "You'll be left with nothing when I am through."

Barnett had the audacity to appear affronted. "Are you mad? Release me at once, Blackwood."

"Not until we have a little chat." He tightened his grip, satisfied when the earl's face turned red. "I want to know what possessions remain from the former earl's family, what you haven't yet sold off to cover your debts, you miserable worm."

"Everything here belongs to me," he rasped.

Lucien leaned in. "While that may be true in a legal sense, I find it difficult to believe there isn't one painting, one knick-knack, one *piece of lint* left over from the former family. I suggest you think hard about it, because I'm not letting you go until I get an answer."

"You have no right—"

"The best part of being a duke is that I have every right to do as I wish with absolute impunity. That includes making men disappear. There's no one to stop me from squeezing the life out of you and dropping your body into the Thames."

Real fear seeped into Barnett's dark eyes as he clawed at Lucien's unforgiving grip on his throat. "Wait, please."

"Have you thought of something?"

"Yes," the earl squeaked. "There's a painting."

Lucien eased his grip, then cast the other man away in disgust. "Then I suggest you go retrieve it for me."

Barnett darted from the room and up the stairs. In case the earl was lying, Lucien decided to give him ten minutes, no more. If Barnet hadn't returned by then, Lucien would follow.

With two minutes to spare the earl hurried down the stairs, a canvas in hand. "Here. Take the damned thing and get out."

Lucien accepted the framed portrait. It was of a young Eliza, Fanny, Robert and their parents. Robert's unhappy expression seemed to stare out at Lucien, a judgmental glare full of resentment.

I'm sorry, Robert. I couldn't resist her.

"Satisfied now, Blackwood?"

Lucien quirked a brow at the insolent earl. "No, not in the least. I won't be satisfied until you are living on scraps, cast out of this home . . .as your cousins were forced to do five years ago. Be forewarned, Barnett. Your debts are coming due." He'd personally see to it that the moneylenders came calling as soon as possible.

Gripping the painting in his fist, Lucien stalked out of the townhouse and found his carriage. During the ride, he braced himself for the sight of Eliza again. Today was their last day together, and he had to find a way to let her go.

It was why he'd avoided her for three and a half days. The more time he spent with her, the more he wanted to keep her—and that was out of the question. Someday she'd learn what happened to her brother and she would hate Lucien for it. The best course of action would be to pay her and let her start over, return her life to some normalcy. Then they could all forget the last five years ever happened.

The ride to his townhouse took hardly any time at this early hour, which was why he was surprised to see people gathered on his stoop.

It was Eliza...and Rathbone. The marquess stood a bit too close to Eliza, as if he was using his body to intimidate her.

Lucien was out of the carriage before the wheels even stopped rolling. "Rathbone," he barked. "Move away from her."

Eliza appeared relieved to see him, which meant Rathbone had been harassing her again.

"Duke, you're just in time," Rathbone drawled.

Lucien headed straight for the pair, painting in hand. "To pulverize you into a jelly? Excellent. Been looking forward to it."

"No, to hear me inform her ladyship about her brother."

A sinking feeling bloomed in Lucien's gut, but he shoved it aside. Only a few people knew what happened that night, and none would betray him by discussing it. Rathbone was clearly referring to something else.

"My brother?" Eliza's brows arched. "What about him?"

Rathbone's voice was sharp, like a blade, cutting and clipped. "Hasn't His Grace informed you what happened the night your brother was killed?"

"Shut your mouth," Lucien snapped as panic lit up his insides. He didn't want anyone to hear this, especially Eliza. She'd never think of him the same way again. "There's no need to dredge up those old memories for her."

"No, wait," Eliza said. "I want to hear it. Please, my lord. What about my brother?"

"Eliza, go inside," Lucien ordered. "Allow me to speak with Rathbone alone."

She never even looked at him, her attention remaining on the marquess.

Malice glittered in Rathbone's dark eyes, his lips curled into a gleeful smirk. "She deserves to know, Blackwood, especially since you were determined to win her from me the other night and make me look like a fool. Or were you planning on keeping the part you played in Robert's death a secret from her forever?"

CHAPTER 10

*E*liza studied both men. She didn't trust Rathbone, but Lucien appeared on edge, his body trembling as if he might strike the marquess at any minute.

Which made her wonder—again—if he had something to hide.

Had Lucien something to do with Robert's death?

Rathbone had appeared this morning outside Lucien's house when she arrived, clearly having followed her. Without preamble, he asked how well she knew Lucien. When she tried to escape inside, Rathbone carried on, insisting on speaking with her. That was when Lucien had arrived.

So, what was really going on?

"Your Grace?" she prompted when Lucien didn't say anything. "Care to explain?"

Instead, Lucien glared at Rathbone. "Get off my property."

"Interesting what I was able to learn by digging into your life, Blackwood. Your former mistresses do like to talk."

Lucien took a threatening step forward, but the marquess held up his hands and bowed to her. "My lady, when you leave him—and you definitely will—please know you have an admirer in me. I would be more than willing to step into his shoes and set you up in a fine house—"

Bile rose in her throat at the offer, but she was spared the need to respond because Lucien shoved Rathbone toward his carriage. "Get the bloody hell out of here!"

Rathbone smiled slyly and departed, his carriage soon rolling away from Lucien's, but she didn't move. She couldn't. Her feet were rooted to the walk. "Please tell me what he's talking about."

"Come inside and we'll talk."

"Lucien, now."

He rubbed his eyes and sighed. "Eliza, please. I don't wish to do this on the street."

Because he knew it would upset her?

A knot tightened between her shoulder blades, but she marched up the walk, climbed the steps, and went inside. Lucien followed, a painting in his hands. She didn't care much about art at the moment. She'd rather hear what Lucien knew regarding Robert's death.

"We'll talk in my office." Lucien led the way, the house eerily quiet.

Once there, he set the painting on the floor, leaning against his desk. The lines on his face had deepened, making him appear older than his years, and a strange ringing started in her ears. Almost as if her body was warning her of oncoming doom.

"Tell me it isn't true," she said. "Tell me you had nothing to do with my brother's death."

"Eliza . . . ."

"I want the truth. The police were never able to give us much information. I have no idea what happened to him, other than he was robbed and dumped in an alley."

He gestured to the armchairs. "Shall we sit?"

"No, Lucien. Open your gob and speak, man. What happened to Robert?"

He dragged in a deep breath, then let it out slowly. "I was having an affair with an actress. I didn't know it, but this actress was also seeing another man, a dangerous thug who ran one of the waterfront gangs. He found out about her relationship with me and decided to kill me—a fact I was unaware of."

He stared at the wall, his tone even. Like he was reciting a lesson in class. "One night, Robert begged me to attend some dinner party with him, but I cancelled at the last minute. The men from the gang were waiting for Robert when he left the dinner party. They . . .thought he was me. He was shoved into a carriage, beaten, and killed near the docks."

Disbelief and horror washed through her, the news worse than she'd imagined. Still, it didn't make sense. "They thought he was you? Why?"

He cleared his throat as he clasped his hands. "Back then, the three of us . . . We played tricks on one another, especially with women. We would sometimes assume another's identity and misbehave."

A boulder-sized lump settled in her throat. She whispered, "So, this particular woman. You told her . . .?"

"I told her my name was Robert Hartsford, Earl of Barnett."

Eliza doubled over, a hand to her stomach as she nearly crumpled to the floor. He rushed toward her, but she backed away, her palms out as if to ward off an evil spirit. "Do not touch me. God, Lucien! How could you do such a terrible thing? To your best friend? What is *wrong* with you?"

"We did it all the time, Jasper and Robert too. We laughed about it, considered it a big joke."

"I cannot believe this." The backs of her lids burned, the betrayal slashing deep through her heart. Lucien, her kind and serious hero, was no hero at all. He didn't deserve her love, not by a long shot. "I cannot believe you kept this from me, that you would let Fanny and I struggle for years knowing you were responsible. Never once did you try to find us. He died and you went back to your two mistresses and your perfect life on Grosvenor Square."

"I've regretted Robert's death every single second, Eliza. The guilt has weighed on me for five years. But you must believe me, I had no idea you and Fanny had been turned out on the street. I thought you were in Scotland! I would have helped you, I swear."

She scrubbed her face with her hands. "There were nights we ate garbage, slept in alleys. I cleaned privies and shoveled horse shit. Washed clothes and—" She bit off the words and shook her head. "Why am I bothering? You have no idea what it's like to worry, to live without all this." She waved her hand to indicate his home. "You've never had to struggle a day in your life."

"I'm terribly, terribly sorry, Eliza. I would give anything to go back and change things. I never thought any of this would happen. I never wanted anyone to suffer."

"And yet we have." A tear escaped her lids and rolled down her cheek. "We all have, my entire family. You destroyed us." Her voice broke. God, she had *loved* this man, admired and worshipped him. She let him inside her body. All the while he'd known this terrible secret and hadn't shared it.

"That's why I want you to take the money. Please, you needn't clean privies or shovel shit any longer. You can buy a house in Mayfair and forget all of this ever happened."

Was he serious? "I can't do that."

"Why not? You'll be independently wealthy, with a home of your own. Everything you've ever wanted."

I wanted you.

No, she'd wanted the version of Lucien that existed in her head. The real man was cruel and selfish. No wonder he'd been so eager to pay her off and have her disappear! It was the easiest way to reduce his guilt. He thought money would fix this, would give her and Fanny the means to go back in time. To the way things were five years ago.

But life didn't work that way.

"This cannot be fixed with money. You merely want to ease your guilt—but nothing can bring my brother back or erase the last five years."

"I know it won't bring him back, but I'd like to take care of you. I want to get you out of Shoreditch and back where you belong."

And he thought she belonged in Mayfair? "Lucien, I haven't belonged here in a very long time, even when Robert was alive. When I told him my plans to attend university, he ridiculed me. Women are not supposed to be clever here. They're supposed to marry young and fade into the background of their husbands' lives. A forgotten footnote in the sands of time. I don't want that. I've never wanted that."

"Then what do you want? Why did you need the money so desperately if not to change your circumstances?"

He appeared confused, absolutely befuddled that she didn't wish to rejoin his fragile and restrictive world. Frustrated, she snapped, "Because my sister is sick. I need money to take her to a sanitarium in America and help her get better."

"America! You cannot go there. It's . . . ."

"It's, what? Too uncivilized for Your Grace? Too progressive? Too modern?"

"No, it's too far," he shouted, then he immediately closed his eyes as if he regretted the outburst. "I cannot stand the thought of you so far away from me."

"I see." Nodding in understanding, she folded her arms across her chest. "You'd prefer me in a house in Mayfair, where you'll stop by and visit. A few times a week, perhaps? And I'll give you a key to make it easier? Just admit you hoped to turn me into your third mistress, Lucien."

"No, absolutely not. I never planned to sleep with you. I wanted you to retain your virginity, if you recall."

"But then I seduced you, right? Poor Lucien, always fighting off my advances."

"I didn't say that. Stop twisting what I'm saying." He dragged his hands through his hair. "Eliza, I care about you a great deal. I want—I *need* to make things better for you."

But he didn't love her. He didn't even care for her as a woman, only as a cause. A way to alleviate his suffering and assuage his guilt. She would never be more than a bad reminder to him of the past he'd destroyed.

And while taking his money would help Fanny and her in countless ways, it would also ease his conscience. He didn't deserve that relief.

No, he deserved to suffer, to live with the knowledge of how he'd hurt Eliza and her sister. Forever.

As if he sensed the direction of her thoughts, he jerked open a desk drawer and held up a bank draft. "Here. It's already made out to you. Fifty thousand pounds."

Her chest squeezed at the sight of it, but her anger outweighed everything else. *I will not make this easy for him.*

"Keep your money. I don't want it." She turned and started for the door, the backs of her lids burning with oncoming tears.

"Eliza, don't be ridiculous. You need this money. Moreover, you earned it."

"I don't need a bloody thing from you, Lucien. Not now, not ever."

"Wait!"

Reluctantly, she paused at the door. Escape was close at hand, and she desperately longed for space from him. "What is it?"

"Please, take the check—and take this." He came toward her carrying the painting he'd brought in earlier. "I got it this morning from your old home."

Hadn't he understood her a second ago? "I don't want anything from you."

"But it's yours." He flipped to painting to face her. "It's your family's portrait."

The breath left her chest at the sight of those people, so young and so happy. With no idea of the tragedy about to befall them. She didn't even recognize herself, a pampered Mayfair princess who'd believed anything was possible if one only wanted it badly enough.

Lucien held out the frame like he expected her to take it. She shook her head sadly. "You keep it. I don't care to remember the past. I can't afford to. Goodbye, Lucien."

* * *

Two Weeks Later

. . .

LUCIEN SAT BY THE FOUNTAIN, a basket of walnuts on his lap and a cigar clamped between his teeth. The day stretched out in front of him like all the rest—a gauntlet of misery to endure until he could start drinking. Scotch was the only way to sleep, the only way to forget the past. In the meantime, he stayed mostly outside, away from the memories.

He tossed a nut into the fountain, strangely satisfied by the plunking sound as it hit the water. It sounded like a heartbeat, not that he would know as his heart had stopped beating two weeks ago.

God's teeth, he missed her.

I don't need a bloody thing from you, Lucien. Not now, not ever.

She hated him, and rightfully so. He hated himself, too.

It should've been Lucien beaten, kidnapped, and murdered that night, not Robert. No one would have missed Lucien. He had no family, no siblings. Some distant cousin would've lucked into a dukedom and that would have been that.

Instead, his best friend had died, and Eliza and Fanny had suffered.

There were nights we ate garbage, slept in alleys. I cleaned privies and shoveled shit.

Another nut landed in the water. Everything hurt. He couldn't focus, not even on the accounting she'd started for him. Nearly every room of the house reminded him of her. He was fucking miserable.

A scratch on stone caught his attention but he didn't turn around. Likely his valet come to chastise him for not shaving and bathing. Again. "Go away."

"You'll see me—or at least listen to me."

He jolted, the cigar nearly falling from his mouth. Fanny?

Eliza's sister slid onto the stone bench next to him and tilted her chin toward the basket on his lap. "This seems like a fun game. Is there a point?"

"Why are you here?"

"I cannot talk any sense into my sister, so I thought I would try with you. By the looks of it, however, I'm probably wasting my time."

He threw another nut into the water. No doubt she'd come to hear an apology in person, something he damn well owed her. "I must beg your pardon, Lady Fanny. You have every right to hate me as much as your sister does, but please believe me. I never knew the two of you weren't being looked after."

"Just Fanny will do, and thank you for the apology." They sat in silence for a few minutes before she said, "I suppose it's difficult for you to understand why we didn't seek help after our cousin kicked us out, but young women in our world are conditioned to believe no one gives a damn about them. We're hidden away until it's time to marry, kept ignorant of things that really matter. Perhaps we could've found a distant relative to take us in or gone to an orphanage, but Eliza didn't want us separated. It was easier to stay together and find work to support ourselves. Unfortunately, I grew sick and the burden soon fell on Eliza's shoulders alone."

A sharp pain lanced his chest. "I would have given a damn. I *do* give a damn."

"Then why did you let her go?"

"What do you mean? She left."

"And you let that stop you?" She scoffed. "Your Grace, you give up far too easily. Your best friend dies, and you shirk your responsibilities to the estate. Eliza leaves you and you just let her go, willing to watch the best woman you'll ever meet move away and start a life on another continent without you. Do you never fight for anything?"

"I . . ."

The protest died on his tongue. Had he?

Life had come easily to him before Robert's death. Women, friends, the title and wealth—all of it had fallen into Lucien's lap. When the worst had happened to Robert, Lucien had retreated, horrified and embarrassed. He wasn't strong, like Eliza. He was a terrible person, selfish. A reprobate with two mistresses and money he didn't deserve.

He shook his head and threw another walnut in the water. This self-reflection was giving him a headache. "She made it very clear when she left. She doesn't care to see me again."

"Her feelings are hurt. She's angry. Surely you can understand why."

"Of course, I understand. I don't expect her to forgive me."

"So, you won't even try?"

He wouldn't even begin to know how. Hell, he couldn't forgive himself, so how could he expect Eliza to? "She's better off."

"If you could see her, you wouldn't say so."

"Why? What's wrong?" He sat straighter, angling to see Fanny's face. "Is she all right?"

"No, you idiot. She's heartbroken. She's in love with you."

In love with him? The idea was laughable. They hadn't even been reunited for a full week, and nearly all that time he'd been withholding a terrible secret. "No, she's not."

"For a smart man, you are truly thick-headed, Your Grace. *Yes*, she is in love with you. Otherwise, she wouldn't be walking around looking like a creature from a Mary Shelley novel—"

Fanny began coughing then, deep racking coughs that made his own lungs hurt in sympathy. When she quieted, he said, "Shall I fetch you water or tea?"

"No, I'm fine."

"Is it consumption?"

"No. It's some mysterious lung ailment, worsened by the dirty air." She lifted a shoulder. "But everyone fears I'm consumptive, so I try to stay at home."

"This is why she plans to take you to America."

"Yes, to a sanitarium there."

"There are places like that here, you know."

"I think Eliza prefers the idea of a fresh start. No doubt you could convince her otherwise, if you gave a damn."

Of course he gave a damn. He loved her, for God's sake. Which is why he had to let her go. She was better off without him, building her independent life without memories and judgment. He threw another walnut. "What makes you think I don't?"

"Because you're brooding here instead of telling her how you feel and trying to win her back."

"I've hurt her enough."

"Therefore your guilt is more important than a future with her?"

"Are you saying I shouldn't feel guilty?"

"You most definitely should feel guilty. You should feel awful for being a foolish young man who thought he was impervious to the consequences of his selfishness."

The next nut landed in the water with more vigor, splashing them. "Then you may sleep well at night, because I do."

"We cannot change the past, Your Grace. The present is for the living, the future for our penance. What is your penance?"

"Liver disease and insomnia, if I had to guess."

"Be serious. Free of all that transpired with Robert, do you want her?"

If he hadn't ruined Eliza's life? If Robert were still alive? The answer came instantly. "Yes."

"Then fix it."

She made it sound so easy. "How?"

"That is for you to figure out. You're clever."

The nape of his neck tightened in annoyance. He chucked another nut into the fountain. "Lovely chat. Thank you for dropping by."

She merely chuckled. "I realize it's not the answer you're hoping for, but it's for you to figure out."

"Do you . . . ?" He forced himself to ask it, even if he sounded like a fool. "Do you think she can forgive me after I ruined your lives?"

"You didn't ruin our lives. Robert's death gave us a different life, but we aren't unhappy. We have freedom, while women in Mayfair do not. I think Eliza learned how strong she was, how much we love each other. We wouldn't trade the last five years for anything."

A glimmer of light took root in his dark soul, a seed of hope that Eliza might one day forgive him. That they could live in the present and not the past. "Truly?"

Waving her hand, Fanny said, "Of course, I wish my brother was still alive—I miss him terribly—and I wish I wasn't sick. Our lives, though, have vastly improved since leaving Mayfair. Had Robert lived, we each would've been married off to a man we hardly knew and started having children. Our possessions and our bodies would've belonged to our husbands. Now, though we are poor, everything we have is ours."

Eliza's fierce independence made more sense now. Why on earth would she ever come back to Mayfair, back to him? "When you put it like that, I'm not certain I stand a chance in winning her."

She rose and shook out her skirts. "I have faith in you, Your Grace."

CHAPTER 11

*L*etters began arriving daily.

At first, Eliza stared at Lucien's seal, wary. If they were love notes, she wasn't certain she cared to read them. Two and a half weeks had passed since she saw him last, and she still felt a gnawing anger in her belly when she thought of him.

And an ache in her heart.

So she let the letters collect on the kitchen table. Each night, Fanny would ask, "Are you going to open them today?" To which Eliza would respond, "No."

Finally, when there were more than ten, Fanny apparently decided to take matters into her own hands. After dinner, she reached for one and opened it.

"What are you doing?" Eliza screeched as she dried her hands on a towel. "Leave those alone."

"I will not. I'm dying of curiosity." Fanny unfolded the paper. "Blimey. That's disappointing."

"This is an invasion of my privacy—and don't tell me what's inside. I don't want to know."

"It's not a letter. It's a maths problem."

Surprise had Eliza taking the paper out of her sister's hands. Sure enough, Lucien hadn't written a word. He'd sent her a complicated equation to solve.

How...clever. A smile tugged at her lips before she could hide it.

"Aha!" Fanny playfully smacked the table with her palm. "I saw that reaction—and it's the first time you've smiled in more than two weeks."

"Stop." Eliza set the paper down and returned to the dishes. "It's interesting, is all. I hadn't expected it."

As she washed their plates and cutlery, her mind turned over the problem, working it out in her head. By the time everything was dry, she'd solved it. Her impulse was to share the solution with him, but that was silly. That would require mailing the letter back, and she didn't care to start any epistolary dialogue with him, even of the mathematical kind.

I love the way you make me feel. Never leave me, my clever girl.

Damn him. Why had he said things such as that, sweet things that caused her to fall in love with him again, while hiding information about Robert's death?

The paper on the table beckoned, her hand itching to write the solution down. Of course, she could write the answer but never mail the letter back to him. Yes, that's what she'd do. She would do this for *her*, not for him.

Taking a pencil, she sat at the table and scribbled. Fanny said nothing, just watched, until Eliza finished. "Quite impressive," her sister said. "Are you going to send it to him?"

"No."

Eliza reached to open another letter. As she suspected, it contained a different problem. This one was simpler, and she was reaching for a third letter in no time.

At some point Fanny drifted away, but Eliza kept at it. When she opened and solved all ten letters, it was quite late. A familiar sense of accomplishment fluttered in her chest. It felt nice. She hadn't done that in quite awhile.

"Are you going to forgive him?" Fanny, dressed in her nightgown, strolled over and sat at the table. "Because he obviously misses you."

"I'm not certain that's true. It's not as if he poured his heart out in the letters."

"Yes, he did." Fanny rolled her eyes toward the ceiling. "Eliza, he thought up these problems, wrote them down, and sent them to you. Maths is your thing."

"Our thing?"

"Your poetry. Your flowers and valentines. Come on. Can you not see it? The man is wildly in love with you."

Eliza shook her head. "You're wrong, and I don't wish to discuss it."

"Do you hate him for the role he played in Robert's death?"

Did she? Certainly, it had been selfish on Lucien's part to pose as another, but he admitted the three friends had laughed about it. Robert and Jasper had used other names, as well.

Still, Lucien hadn't told her, not even after sleeping with her. If it weren't for Rathbone, she never would've learned what happened.

But did she hate Lucien?

No. God, no. It would be far easier if she did, if these feelings lingering inside her disappeared. Loving him was terrible, painful and awful, like a rotten tooth she wished she could extract. Instead, the ache remained, twisting her up into knots.

"I don't hate him, but he hurt me. It's unforgivable."

"Unforgivable? Really, Eliza? That seems harsh, considering."

"Considering, what? That he was responsible for Robert's death and never told me? I trusted him with my body and my heart, and he has proven unworthy of that trust."

"Yes, he should've told you before taking you to bed, but can you honestly say you gave him a chance? You said you seduced him each time."

"Believe it or not, we did have conversations outside of bed, too."

Fanny coughed, then took a moment to catch her breath. Eliza waited patiently, hating that her sister struggled. *Maybe I should've taken Lucien's money.*

No, they would find another way. They always did.

When Fanny spoke, it was quieter. "You cannot fault him for what came after Robert's death or for my illness."

"I know." Eliza rolled the pencil on the table, not wanting to meet Fanny's eye. "I shouldn't have made Lucien think I blamed him for our financial straits."

"No, you shouldn't have. You know we're happier now, together and poor, than we ever would've been as separated, married, and rich ladies."

"Yes, but your illness," Eliza said. "That's because of where we live, these conditions."

"Dr. Humphries isn't certain about that. He said I might have caught it somewhere, or I might've been born with it and it took this long to present. The truth is, we don't know."

"I suppose. Why are you pushing me to give Lucien another chance, anyway?"

"Because I want to see you happy—and you were happy during that one week. It was clearly Lucien's doing."

"I won't be his mistress, and there aren't other options for a girl like me."

"Why not? You'd make a fine duchess."

"Sure. Can't you see me in Mayfair, telling all those fine ladies about my various jobs over the years? Not to mention auctioning off my virginity. I'd fit right in over petit fours."

"You're embarrassed of how you've earned a living for us."

"No, I'm not," she snapped. "I worked my bloody tail off to support us, and neither one of us had to—"

"Sell our bodies?" Fanny finished when Eliza fell silent.

Eliza grimaced. Yes, that was what she'd been about to say.

Fanny yawned and stretched her arms. "Who cares about what people say? You never have up until now."

"You merely wish for me to end up with Lucien, like I'm Cinderella or some such nonsense. You're making it sound so easy when we both know it's not."

"It won't be easy, but you're the strongest, most determined person

I know. If you want something bad enough, you'll bring it about come hell or high water. The question is, what do you want?"

Eliza considered it, but her emotions were too jumbled, too scattered to come up with an answer about Lucien. She focused on the two of them, instead. "I want you to get better. I want to take you to America so you can recover."

"At some point, you need to live for yourself. I'll be fine. Don't ruin your chance at happiness for me."

"I love you. I'm not ruining anything by taking care of you. You're my family."

Fanny reached forward to clutch Eliza's hand. "We'll always be family. But I also know we need more than just each other. You might not want them, but I do want a husband and children."

This was the first they'd ever discussed it. "So, what are you saying? You want me to send you to America by yourself?"

"Perhaps. I don't know."

It was only fair, but the prospect caused sorrow to scald the back of Eliza's throat. She couldn't imagine a life without Fanny in it.

Exhaustion weighed her down. Lord, it was after one o'clock, and such a conversation was too heavy for this hour. She stood. "I have an early morning, so I'll go to bed. Are you coming?"

"In a bit. I want to get some water first."

"All right. Good night."

Once she was in bed, Eliza told herself not to think about Lucien. Not to miss him or to wonder what he was doing.

Her resolve quickly crumbled in the darkness, however, and she fell asleep to memories of his filthy words and possessive touch.

* * *

"A LETTER ARRIVED FOR YOU TODAY," Fanny said as soon as Eliza walked in the door from work. Fanny grinned. "Several letters, actually."

Eliza didn't want to admit it, but her heart leapt at the news. The letters from Lucien had continued, even a week later, and she looked forward to them. One might even have said they were the highlight of her day.

She strove for nonchalance. "Oh?"

"And they're not all from Lucien."

That got Eliza's attention. "Please don't tell me it's from a bill collector."

"Don't be absurd. We're current on all of our payments." Fanny held up a very fancy looking letter. "This is from Somerville College."

"At Oxford?" Eliza's brows climbed as high as they could go. "Who is it for?"

"You, silly." Fanny rushed over and handed Eliza the letter. "I didn't open it. I wanted to, very, very badly, but I didn't."

"Thanks, Fan," Eliza drawled. There was no privacy between two sisters who lived together.

"Open it!"

Eliza opened the letter and then gaped. "It's from Mrs. Maitland, the principal."

"Cor," Fanny whispered. "What does she say?"

Eliza read quickly. Apparently, Mrs. Maitland had reviewed the maths solutions Eliza had sent and invited her to sit for Somerville's entrance exam next term.

"Oh, my God," Eliza breathed. "I've been invited to sit for the entrance exam at Somerville College."

"You're going to Oxford?" Fanny screamed.

Eliza looked at Mrs. Maitland's words again. Wait, what maths solutions? And she'd never written to Somerville. "This doesn't make any sense."

A guilty look crossed Fanny's face as she twined her fingers together. A sure sign of nerves. "What have you done?" Eliza asked her sister.

"Nothing! I returned those solutions to Blackwood. After that, I never saw them again. You'll have to ask him what he did with them."

Eliza pinched the bridge of her nose between her thumb and forefinger. "Lucien. I should've known."

The man couldn't help himself.

Even though she'd refused his money and assistance, he'd gone and done *this*. He must've sent those sheets of paper to Mrs. Maitland and begged the principal to take Eliza on. How embarrassing.

"Wait, why are you frowning? This is exciting, Liza."

"I suppose, but I can't go." She folded the principal's letter and set it on the table.

"Whyever not?"

"First, no doubt Lucien has paid the woman to make the offer to me. Second, we cannot afford it. Third, I cannot leave you to fend for yourself."

"Lucien wouldn't do that, and there are charity societies who could cover your costs. And if you're concerned about me, you needn't worry any longer." Fanny held out another letter, this one addressed to her.

"What's this?"

"Read it," Fanny urged.

Eliza took the paper. Her breath caught at the name on the outside. "The Royal National Hospital for Chest Diseases?"

Fanny's grin took up almost her entire face. "They've accepted me. I'm leaving for the Isle of Wight tomorrow."

"Tomorrow!" To mask her rioting emotions, Eliza quickly read the letter. Sure enough, Fanny had been given a treatment bed there and they would send someone to escort her to the hospital tomorrow. "I can't believe this."

"It's a bleedin' miracle. They only take thirty or so patients a year. And my fees have been paid."

"It's not a miracle. It's the Duke of Blackwood."

"I don't care. I'm not stupid enough to turn down an opportunity like this."

The comment dug under Eliza's ribs like a sharp knife. "And you think I am? Stupid enough to turn down Oxford, that is?"

Fanny sighed. "I don't think you're stupid. I think you're proud and stubborn, and in the past I've always agreed with you. Someone without your best interests at heart will try to take advantage, but that isn't the case here. Lucien has your best interests at heart. Can't you see? He's in love with you. He's trying to make things better for you without gaining anything in return."

In love with her? The idea was ludicrous. "Wrong. No doubt he expects me to . . . ."

"To what? Go to Oxford and study until your brain melts? He's not even trying to keep you in London, Liza. He's giving you a life without him in it. How is that possibly serving his own interests?"

"He's doing this because he feels guilty."

"And? Why do you think rich nobs give to charities? To ease their guilt." Fanny shook her head, clearly frustrated. "Do you think for one second I am going to turn down the opportunity to recuperate at this prestigious hospital because I'm worried about easing Lucien's guilt?"

"No, and I wouldn't let you. This is a tremendous opportunity for you."

Fanny gestured to the letter from Mrs. Maitland. "This is no different."

"Wrong. Going to study at Oxford isn't life or death."

"Isn't it? If you stay here, you'll work yourself to the bone for the rest of your days. If you go off to school, everything will change for the better. This will change the course of your life."

"For which I will owe him."

"Who solved those maths problems every night? Who will have to pass the entrance exams?"

"That is hardly—"

"Who?" Fanny repeated.

"Me, but—"

"There is no but. You proved your worth on those pieces of paper. You deserve this. You deserve to go. You owe no one for your intelligence. He merely helped you illustrate it to the right people."

Ever so slowly, the heaviness sitting on her chest began to lift. Was Fanny right? Did Eliza deserve this? Biting her lip to contain her hopeful smile, she stared at Mrs. Maitland's letter. Could she really sit for the entrance exams?

It seemed almost too good to be true.

Was it more than guilt on Lucien's part? Fanny thought the duke was in love with Eliza, but he'd barely hinted at deeper feelings whilst they were together.

I cannot stand the thought of you so far away from me.

Yet he was helping her leave London to study in Oxford.

She couldn't think about this right now. Apparently, Fanny was departing in the morning and Eliza needed to help her sister prepare. There would be time to contemplate her own life later.

CHAPTER 12

"I don't care what it costs," Lucien snapped at Mr. Paulson, the architect. "We cannot throw these people out on the streets. Offer them twice the fair market value and do not bully them."

"Your Grace," Paulson started. "With all due respect, this sets a terrible precedent for other—"

"That is not my problem. If these families won't sell, we'll find another property."

"Very well. I'll see to it personally." He started to collect the plans, but Lucien held out a hand.

"I'd like to review those drawings. Leave them with me and I'll see them returned tomorrow."

The architect blinked several times behind his spectacles. "You wish to review the plans?" At Lucien's nod, Paulson said, "Shall I explain them to you first? They can be rather complicated to the untrained eye."

"I'll manage." Lucien struggled to keep his tone polite in the face of the architect's condescension. "My man will see you out."

Lucien's new secretary rose from where he'd been taking notes and escorted Paulson out of the office. Standing, Lucien spread the plans for the settlement house on his desk. Hartsford Hall would be a place to offer food, shelter, and education to poor women and girls. They were searching for the right location, though he was leaning toward the Old Nichol, a notorious slum situated between Shoreditch and Bethnal Greene.

"Your Grace, a visitor."

Lucien glanced up to tell his butler to refuse any caller—and the words died in his throat.

Eliza.

She was there, standing tall and beautiful, a vision straight out of one of his dreams. His mouth dried out and he couldn't think of a thing to say, lest he scare her off somehow. Was she truly here?

He drank in her fine features and golden hair. The lithe curves barely visible under her garments. Her cheeks held a slight flush, her lips plump and red, as if she had been biting them. Goddamn, he missed her.

She nodded at his butler and came closer, her skirts rustling, and his butler pulled the door shut. "Hello, Your Grace."

He hated the formality, loathed the distance between them, but he had no one to blame but himself. Though he ached to take her into his arms and kiss the living hell out of her, he forced a smile and folded his hands behind his back. "Lady Eliza. To what do I owe the pleasure?"

"May I sit?"

"Of course." He came forward to help assist her, but she waved him away. He would accept her independence or be damned.

His chest twisted, his insides raw and tattered. He'd screwed everything up from the start, and he deserved the misery now permanently lodged in his heart.

Clearing his throat, he lowered himself into his chair. "You look well."

"I've come to thank you."

Straight and to the point, as always. He wanted to grin, but his face hadn't attempted one in six weeks. He wasn't certain he was capable of it any longer.

Besides, she was only here to thank him for Fanny and the Royal

Hospital. A small sliver of disappointment dug under his skin, but he pushed it aside. What had he expected? That she'd missed him, as he'd missed her?

He held her gaze. "That wasn't necessary."

"Indeed, it is. You've given Fanny the very best hope for recovery. I'm entirely grateful."

"She's left already?"

"Yes, yesterday."

He nodded once. Good. The hospital was the best in Europe and if anyone could heal Eliza's sister, it was those doctors. "I'm happy to hear it."

"I admit, it wasn't easy to let her go." She gave a small laugh, as if she knew it was silly. "We haven't been apart for five years. I felt like a mama bird watching her baby leave the nest."

"They'll take very good care of her."

"I know. Whatever your reasons for helping us, I cannot begin to thank you enough."

He didn't want her gratitude. He wanted her laughter and kisses. The touch of her hand across his bare skin. He wanted to roll over every morning and see her face beside him, then finish the day by solving problems together before taking her to bed.

I love you, he almost said. *I would do anything for you.*

But she would never believe his motives were pure. She would always think he was trying to rid himself of his guilt or control her through privilege and money.

He nodded once, unable to think of anything more brilliant to say other than, "You're welcome."

"I leave for Oxford next month. I thought you'd like to know."

Straightening, he blurted, "Oxford?"

"Come now. Surely you were aware."

"Aware of what, exactly?"

"I've heard from Mrs. Maitland. About sitting for the entrance exams."

"At Somerville College? Eliza, that's tremendous. Congratulations."

"I have you to thank for that, as well."

"Why? Because I sent her the problems you solved?"

"Yes, and asked her to take me on as a student."

"I did no such thing." When her expression didn't change, he leaned forward. "Eliza, I didn't bribe her or pay her to offer you a spot, if that's what you mean. I merely sent her the problems along with your address. I didn't even affix my seal to the letter."

Her mouth parted. "You didn't wield your ducal influence?"

"Not with Mrs. Maitland. I admit I did so with the Royal Hospital, however."

"You mean...."

"You did that all on your own, Eliza. Because you're brilliant and tenacious. I couldn't be prouder."

"I can't believe it," she murmured, rubbing her forehead. "I thought for certain it was because of you."

Remaining silent, the truth began to sink in. Hope and happiness were pushed aside as his own thoughts turned darker. Even if she forgave him, she would go away to study and live apart from him. Build a life free from the horrors of her past, including him. It was what he'd always wanted for her, except he hadn't expected it to hurt this badly.

When she finally looked up, her eyes were moist. "I don't know what to say."

"It's very happy news." For her, anyway. "You're allowed to be overwhelmed."

"No, that's not what I meant." She exhaled slowly. "To you. I don't know what to say to you."

"Oh." He lifted his shoulders and let them fall. "I don't quite know what to say to you, either, other than I'm dashed proud of you and I wish you all the very best. You're going to have a marvelous time."

"Part of me doesn't want to go."

"Why on earth not? You no longer have Fanny to look after. You may do anything you like now."

"I don't want to go because...well, because you won't be there."

His muscles jolted, the words hitting him square in the chest. Had she missed him? Was she entertaining the idea of a future with him? "What are you saying?"

"I can't stop thinking about you. About us. I miss you."

"God, Eliza." He closed his eyes briefly. "I miss you so much. I'm miserable without you."

"Then why haven't you told me?"

"I did. With the letters. I thought . . . ." He thought she'd understand what he was doing.

"I knew you were thinking of me and trying to get my attention, but I want to hear what's in your heart. I need the words, Lucien."

Do you never fight for anything?

Remembering Fanny's words, Lucien swallowed his nerves and stood. In a few steps, he reached Eliza's chair, where he took her arm, pulled her to her feet, and cupped her face in his hands. "I love you madly, Eliza. I love everything about you, from your clever brain to your stubborn will. I want you here with me, by my side, until I draw my last breath."

A tear slipped free from the corner of her eye. "Even after everything I've done for the last five years? After offering up my virginity to a room full of strangers?"

He gently brushed the tear away with his fingers. "Do you still want me after everything I've done to you, to your family? I kept a terrible secret from you, and let you suffer on the streets."

"Yes, I do. We can't change the past, and my brother deserves his fair share of the blame for not providing for Fanny and me. But you need to be sure about how you feel, because the whispers will dog me for the rest of my life if I stay in London."

"Let them whisper. It's because of all you've done that I love you. There's no one stronger than you, no one who needs rescuing less than you. You don't need me, but I hope like hell that you want me, because I need you so desperately, angel."

"I love you. And I do want you, but I'm not certain this world is one in which I fit any longer."

He shook his head. "You'll fit in wherever you go. And besides, I thought we were moving to Oxford."

"You would move to Oxford for me?"

"You make that sound like a hardship. I wasn't jesting, Eliza. I need you by my side, day in and day out. I don't care where."

"Even if we never come back to Mayfair?"

"I don't give a fuck about Mayfair."

A spark flashed through her blue gaze at his profanity. Then she rose up on her toes and sealed her lips to his. He wasted no time in kissing her deeply, the sensation washing over him like rain on a barren desert. He'd missed the feel of her mouth, the soft stroke of her tongue. He would never get enough.

When they broke for air, she whispered, "There's that filthy mouth I like so much."

"You may have it whenever you desire."

"What about now?"

A blast of heat bored through his system, filling every pore and cell with lust for her. "Sit on my desk and lift your skirts so I may lick you and make you come on my tongue. Then you'll agree to marry me."

Her hooded gaze darkened. "Yes, Your Grace."

Edging around his desk, she looked down and paused. "What's this?" She was staring at the plans for the settlement house. "Hartsford Hall?"

He removed his topcoat and tossed it onto an armchair. "A settlement house I'm building in Shoreditch."

"You . . .what?" Head lowered, she trailed her fingers over the plans. "This is amazing, Lucien."

"It's nothing. The very least I can do." After removing his cufflinks, he began unbuttoning his vest. "On the desk, my sweet girl."

The edge of her mouth lifted as she took him in. "Sit down, Your Grace."

"What?"

She pointed to his chair. "Right now."

He liked this bossy side of her. Crossing to his heavy leather armchair, he asked, "Why?"

After he sat, she lowered herself to her knees. Lucien's lungs seized as she reached for the fastenings on his trousers, her fingers skimming his hard cock. "I feel like I need another lesson. And I promise to be a very diligent student for you."

"Oh, Jesus," he gasped, her palm pressing hard on the ridge of his shaft and sending a jolt of pleasure down to his toes. "You're sure?"

"Very." She bit her lip and stared up at him through her lashes. "And you know what studying at Somerville College means, don't you?"

He swallowed. "No, what?"

"I will have access to many, many rulers."

* * *

Thank you for reading *Sold to the Duke*!

If you like your historical romance short and spicy, make sure to check out MY DIRTY DUKE, my age-gap bang-fest!

* * *

Violet knows that her father's best friend, the Duke of Ravensthorpe, is the most powerful man in all of London with a reputation for sin.

But nothing can stop Violet from wanting to shed her wallflower ways and fulfill her darkest, most forbidden desires…even if it means seducing a man twice her age.

"Shupe is a true queen of filth, expert at spinning heartfelt love stories alongside tantalizingly wicked scenarios."
—*Entertainment Weekly*

Click here to read *My Dirty Duke*
for free in Kindle Unlimited
or buy the eBook direct on Amazon.

ACKNOWLEDGMENTS

Thank you for reading my virgin auction story!

I had a lot of help along the way, mostly from the I'd Like to F… crew: Sierra Simone, Eva Leigh, Nicola Davison, and Adriana Herrera. The anthologies may not exist any longer, but they live on in our hearts (and in our Slack channel!). Love these smart writers.

Hugs and kisses to the fabulous Diana Quincy, who always makes time for me, even when I'm a nuisance.

Letitia Hasser at RBA Designs killed it once again with this fabulous cover. And thank you to Sabrina Darby, who helped me shape this story into something readable.

And thanks to Mr. Shupe, who said the ending of STTD made him tear up! He's the best partner, line editor, plot fixer, and all around best.

ALSO BY JOANNA SHUPE

Fifth Avenue Rebels:

The Heiress Hunt

The Lady Gets Lucky

The Bride Goes Rogue

The Uptown Girls:

The Rogue of Fifth Avenue

The Prince of Broadway

The Devil of Downtown

The Four Hundred Series:

A Daring Arrangement

A Scandalous Deal

A Notorious Vow

The Knickerbocker Club:

Tycoon

Magnate

Baron

Mogul

Wicked Deceptions:

The Courtesan Duchess

The Harlot Countess

The Lady Hellion

Novellas:

How The Dukes Stole Christmas Anthology

Miracle on Ladies' Mile

My Dirty Duke

ABOUT THE AUTHOR

USA Today bestselling author **Joanna Shupe** has always loved history, ever since she saw her first Schoolhouse Rock cartoon. Since 2015, her books have appeared on numerous yearly "best of" lists, including *Publishers Weekly*, *The Washington Post*, *Kirkus Reviews*, Kobo, and BookPage.

Sign up for Joanna's Gilded Lilies Newsletter for book news, sneak peeks, reading recommendations, historical tidbits, and more!

www.joannashupe.com

Printed in Great Britain
by Amazon